Mulligans

By Charlie David

Chase never had many friends, but at college, he meets and forms close ties with straight jock Tyler Davidson—a connection he fears he'll lose if he tells Tyler he's gay. Keeping his sexuality secret becomes harder for Chase as he joins Tyler and his family at their idyllic lake house for the summer. It grows more and more difficult for Chase to avoid Tyler's attempts to set him up with girls, and he's tired of making excuses. Chase is ready to embrace the man he is, but he's afraid of what it will cost him.

The Davidsons seem like the perfect family, but Chase soon realizes there's trouble in paradise. Tyler's dad, Nathan, has done everything to make a good life for his wife and children—including suppressing his sexuality and denying his needs for years. But like Chase, Nathan is growing weary of living a lie. What begins as an offer of support from Chase grows into an unexpected attraction that will have profound effects on everyone. Chase and the Davidsons are about to learn that there's no such thing as a perfect family and that perfection is overrated.

YOU CAN'T BLAME a person for who they are, Chase thought, leaning against his best friend's car—a new silver Beemer convertible, but who keeps track of things like that? The spring breeze licked its way through the hallway of trees lining the long driveway up to the residential halls of the university. The place was a zoo this morning as parents returned to pick up their sons and daughters for the summer. Chase inwardly winced, just a little. Being the only son of a single mom hardly made him a charity case in this day and age—more run of the mill, actually. What upset him was the look on his peers' faces when they greeted their parents: a look of excitement, a look of anticipation of happy times, laughter, and memories to be made this summer. He'd seen the same look on his classmates every year through grade school, and it was no different now. He wanted to feel that, wanted to manufacture it somehow, but he wasn't even sure where to start. The only part worse than the end of the school year was the beginning of another, when those same faces returned, nearly busting at the seams from their ear-to-ear smiles, competing to outdo each other with stories of their magical summers.

He desperately wanted to feel something, anything, for his own mother, but he just… couldn't. There was nothing there. The closest thing to an emotional response he could identify might be sympathy, but it wasn't that strong. Apathy would be much closer to the mark. Too many years spent watching her drink herself into a stupor. He couldn't blame her. Or could he? No, he was past that. What do you do when the love of your life dies and you're left with a runty kid to raise by yourself? Raise the kid, not another glass…. Enough!

Chase took a deep breath and rechecked the clock on the tall bell tower above the residence hall's front door. Tyler was only slightly later than usual. While waiting, he could easily get lost for hours in the labyrinth of his mind and all the dark corners of his past. But not today. The sun was shining, college was out for the summer, and he and Tyler were going to spend it together. A smile played on his face. At last something to look forward to.

Tyler Davidson was… well, perfect, mostly, except for his habitual lateness, but even that minor fault Chase could readily forgive. His best friend was everything he wasn't, or at least that was the way Chase saw it. Tall, blond, blue-eyed, hunky Tyler. Always ready with a one-liner to make people laugh and seemingly able to glide through life without a care. Girls wanted to be with him and guys wanted to be him. Somehow he'd decided to lay down the unjust title of Best Buddy on Chase—a term that in Chase's mind only served to contrast them further.

It wasn't that Chase wasn't handsome; he was just more of an acquired taste, with short dark hair and big almond eyes. And next to the roaring blaze that lit up a room when Tyler entered it, Chase felt like he was a single burning match, good to light a cigarette occasionally but hardly something to gather around.

He was obsessing again. It was a habit—not a particularly useful one either, just something he'd gotten in, well, the habit of. Chase closed his eyes and took a deep breath, enjoying the feel of the warm sun on his face.

A summer to look forward to, he considered. He had no idea what to expect. When Tyler had asked if he'd like to spend the summer with his family at their lake house, he hadn't even stopped to think before saying yes. Since then, of course, he'd obsessed about it, imagining every detail. It sounded so… exotic: summer at the lake house. Definitely far from his existence in his mother's city apartment.

He'd actually been a little surprised by the ask; they'd only met this year. Chase had transferred to the university on scholarship after working his ass off for the past two years at a subpar community college. He wouldn't have been able to afford the tuition, but fate had smiled on him when he submitted his art portfolio and was invited to attend gratis. Fate had smiled on him again when he and Tyler were assigned to share a dorm room. They had hit it off immediately, but Chase was still at a loss as to what exactly it was that Tyler saw in him. Tyler could have chosen to spend his time with anyone he liked—there was all but a line outside the dorm room every day. But Tyler chose him. He didn't need to understand why; he could just enjoy it.

A summer to look forward to. There it was, a feeling growing inside him. Not manufactured. Real. He couldn't name it yet, but it was there. He smiled, and when he opened his eyes he saw it reflected on his best friend's face as he ran down the front stairs of the dorm, a duffel bag swung over his shoulder.

"You ready?" Tyler asked, beaming his megawatt smile at Chase and tossing the bag atop a pile of others in the backseat of the convertible. "I'm sorry, that took longer than I expected. I'm ready now, for real."

"No worries. I didn't even notice the time," Chase answered as he hopped in the passenger seat. "To summer!"

"To us!"

"To the lake house!"

Tyler revved the engine and pulled into the steady stream of cars exiting the campus. Sunlight danced through the trees lining the driveway. "So I talked to Marty, the owner of the golf course, and we're all set up. We're green gophers for the summer. It's super easy. I did it the past couple years. Anyway, it'll be pocket money for us at school next year, right?"

"Can always use that," Chase answered, feeling the ache of the empty pockets in his jeans.

"Don't worry. I got you covered until payday if you need anything," Tyler said absentmindedly as he drummed his fingers on the steering wheel in time to the music on the radio.

That was part of the problem. Tyler was always paying for Chase. Even with his tuition covered, Chase hadn't quite expected or planned for the additional expenses that could sneak up at university: beer, late-night pizza, weekend trips, concert tickets, and the list went on. And it was never a question—Tyler opened his wallet and magically everything was always paid for. "Don't worry, you're going to be a famous artist one day, and then I'll be asking for free paintings for my house. I got you," Tyler would always say. Don't worry, don't worry, don't worry. Chase wished there was some way he could pay him back now, or return the favor somehow. It was more than a gesture; Tyler looked out for him like a stray animal. No, better than that: he looked out for him like he really loved him. Was that the right word to describe it? Chase had never heard the word before—well, not from another person to him—and he'd certainly never felt the words leave his lips spoken to another. *I love football, I love painting, I love rocky road ice cream,* but never *I love you.*

He was going down a rabbit hole again. Not quite obsessing but certainly stewing, and he was supposed to be enjoying the drive with Tyler, who he realized then was glancing at him, his face twisted into a question mark.

"You off in space again, Chastity?" Tyler elbowed him. "I said Albuquerque."

Chastity. The nickname Tyler had laid on him since his side of the dorm room got less action than... well, it had gotten none. Tyler's, on the other hand, was a regular gigolo's lovefest, with regular cuddling, whispered baby talk, and creaking mattress springs.

"Ends with an *e*.... Ethiopia," Chase finally answered, smirking at Tyler. If there was one area where Chase could run circles around his friend, it was with words.

"You and your *A*s. Come on, give me a break."

"I love *A*s," Chase responded nonchalantly.

"I'll give you an *A*. Asshole." Tyler shot him a playful look over his sunglasses.

"Come on, at least try. I can think of like three places that start with *A* right now."

"Hold on.... America!" Tyler exclaimed and shot one fist into the air as if he had just won the lottery.

"Which one?" Chase asked flatly.

"America, America."

"North or South. You have to be specific, which means naming either North or South. Neither of which begins with an *A*," Chase explained.

Tyler stared out at the highway for a while, the yellow lines stretching in an endless ribbon over the horizon. "Alamo."

"What?"

"The Alamo," Tyler said again.

Chase shook his head. "Historical monuments and museums don't count."

"You just made that up, Chastity!"

"Did not. Cities, states, countries—those are okay. No man-made structures, though. Like, you couldn't say Hoover Dam."

"Cities are man-made," Tyler complained.

"Cities count. They're on maps," Chase explained.

"So if it's on a map it counts?"

"Usually."

"Usually?"

"Fine. You know what? Use the Alamo. Whatever," Chase conceded.

"Fine. I will."

"Fine."

"You have an *O*," Tyler said, pleased with himself for winning the battle.

"Omaha."

"Does that end with an *A*?"

"Yeah." Chase punched Tyler in the arm for emphasis.

"Owwww!" Tyler whined.

"Nope, that doesn't start with an *A* either." He punched Tyler again.

"Charlie horse!" Tyler cried out.

"Nope, that's a *C*." Chase shot him another fist in the bicep.

"Do you want me to pull over right now and kick your ass?" Tyler threatened. "I'll do it!"

As the silver Beemer traced the double yellow lines over the horizon, one thing was certain: Chase wasn't obsessing. He wasn't lost in memories of the past, plans for the future, or questioning who he was. He was simply there, with his best friend, playing a childish game, and there was nowhere he'd rather be.

STACEY DAVIDSON pulled a steaming tray of apple-cinnamon muffins out of the oven and set them on a cooling rack on the counter. She stole a quick glance at her reflection in the kitchen window. At thirty-six she still cut a striking figure in her apricot dress, hair pulled back and makeup understated but thoughtful, just like the rest of her. She pushed back a stray strand of blonde hair from her face with an oven mitt and then rested her mitted hands on her hips, assessing the situation. Apple-cinnamon muffins, his favorite; iced tea; fresh fruit salad; sliced mozzarella; Manchego; and Gouda. Fresh coffee rested in the french press, ready to be poured. "I think we're ready," she whispered to herself. It was just an afternoon snack, but her son and his friend would be hungry when they arrived. It was a good four-hour drive from the university out to the lake. She and the family had only arrived the week before from the city, and she'd been on her feet since—spring cleaning, grocery shopping, and preparing the lake house for another summer.

Stacey grabbed the fruit salad and sliced cheese from the counter and made her way to the kitchen table, where her ten-year-old daughter, Birdy, was fully immersed in role-play with her Barbie dolls. Both naked, Skipper and Ken were engaged in a kind of rescue mission. Birdy positioned Ken to kneel over Skipper with his hands on her chest.

"First. See if the victim is conscious and breathing. 'Can you hear me? Can you hear me?'" Birdy lowered her voice to play Ken. "Second. Call for help in a loud, clear voice. 'Help! Help!' Third. If they are not breathing, check the mouth for anything that might be blocking the airway. Like an apple core or something...."

"Birdy, why are your Barbie people naked? Don't you think they might be more comfortable practicing CPR in clothes?" Stacey asked, setting down the fruit salad and cheese plate.

"They were swimming and Skipper almost drowned!" Birdy answered, her eyes wide with the absolute horror of the situation.

"Nakedness is nothing to be ashamed of, Birdy, but at the dining room table maybe they could at least pop on some swimwear. We're about to have company!" Stacey wheeled around behind Birdy, plucked a hair elastic out of her dress pocket, and then deftly pulled her blonde tresses back into a presentable ponytail.

"I know, I know," Birdy lamented. "Tyler's coming home."

The age difference between Birdy and her brother was nearly eleven years, but every once in a while Stacey felt a twinge of despair as she noticed her little girl growing up. The next seven years would pass all too quickly, and then where would she be? She'd have the graduation and prom to plan for, and then there'd be the excitement of getting ready for college, but after that…. She'd already learned over the past three years with Tyler away at university that his need for her in his life was waning. His first year away at college, they had spoken at least every other night, catching up on his classes and new friends, and she was generally able to calm any fear or worry he might have had, although she was sure Tyler wouldn't want all his friends to know he spoke with his mother that often. Part of becoming a man was breaking away from one's mother; she understood that. Still, that didn't make it easy for her. This past year his calls had become increasingly less frequent. She assumed it had something to do with his new friend, Chase. They seemed to spend all their time together. Obviously he had taken her place in some regards as Tyler's confidant. *That's good, that's normal*, she considered, not completely sure what normal was supposed to be.

From outside appearances the Davidson family seemed to have everything cemented together, but those appearances hadn't come without a lot of work. Sure, they had money now, but it certainly hadn't always been that way. Stacey had worked diligently her entire life to create the perfect family. She was desperate to be the casual envy of her neighbors and to sweep rumors swiftly away from their doorstep. There had been too much whispering to deal with in the beginning. But now was a different time, and all of that was behind them. Stacey now held a quiet pride in her family and her life. She had two beautiful children, two beautiful homes, and there was never a worry or want. All due to her husband, Nathan.

Nathan, the handsome giant who she was well aware was the cause of stirring hearts and fluttering eyelashes at the cocktail parties they regularly attended in the city. Nathan, the successful architect and loving father to her children. Nathan, whom she had known since junior high and who had been her high school sweetheart. Nathan, whom even after all these years she desperately loved. Not that they had a perfect marriage, whatever that was supposed to resemble.

When she took a moment to analyze her life, the creeping suspicion would enter her mind that she was actually lonely. Which was exactly why she sought to minimize those moments. Part of the problem, she realized, was that whoever she had once been, she had lost somewhere a very long time ago. Stacey had her interests, but then again, they generally focused on the service of others, namely her family. She enjoyed cooking. She enjoyed taking Birdy to her various extracurricular activities. She was always busy with the continual updating of the family photo albums, and scrapbooking their memories had developed into a frequent hobby. But once Birdy grew up and left... what exactly would she do? She couldn't even really recall what she had enjoyed doing before the kids came along. She'd been so young then. She remembered that she'd enjoyed playing basketball. How utterly absurd the thought was. Basketball. At her age? Where exactly would she find a group of women in their late thirties to play basketball with? She laughed in spite of herself. Besides, she hadn't even been on a court in decades.

Stacey caught herself still standing behind Birdy and staring at the wood grain on the tabletop as her mind rambled. She bent over and kissed the top of Birdy's head. "Please don't grow up too quickly." She whispered a silent prayer to herself.

Just then her husband walked into the dining room. "Mmm... something smells good. Apple-cinnamon muffins, my favorite." Nathan grabbed the newspaper off the counter and settled into his chair at the head of the table. "Birdy, why are your Barbie people naked?"

"They were swimming and Skipper almost drowned!" Birdy repeated for her father's benefit.

"What's on your agenda, Nathan?" Stacey asked, trying to penetrate through the newspaper.

"Once the boys arrive, I thought maybe we'd go out for eighteen holes. You?" Nathan responded without lowering his headlines.

"Birdy has her swimming lesson this afternoon, so we'll be going down to the beach after lunch."

Birdy interrupted her parents nonchalantly. "I saw Jeffrey's penis."

Nathan slowly dropped his paper to the table. "Who is Jeffrey and why have you seen his... um, penis?" Nathan asked, his eyes on Stacey, the question seemingly directed at her instead of Birdy.

"He shows it to me under the water at swimming lessons," she explained as Nathan and Stacey spoke the silent eye language particular to parents and fought to deflect the responsibility of dealing with their daughter's unfortunate anatomy lesson. Both sighed with relief as Tyler and Chase burst through the door.

"Tyler! You're early! Birdy, look, your brother's home!" Stacey exclaimed, running to give Tyler a hug.

"I can see him," Birdy responded casually, with a wave at her brother from the table.

"You must be Chase! We've heard so much about you. Sounds like you two had a lot of fun this year," Stacey said as she wrapped Chase in a hug he didn't seem to expect. "Come in, come in! This is Tyler's sister, Birdy."

Birdy assessed Chase from head to toe before informing him, "I've got a swimming test today. If you need saving while you're here, I could probably do it."

"Cool, I'll keep that in mind." Chase laughed.

"And this is Mr. Davidson." Stacey guided Chase over to a seat near the end of the table.

"Nathan," her husband corrected, extending his hand to shake.

"Of course, we're all adults here. I'm Stacey." She watched as the two men shook hands. There really was no other way to describe Chase; he was a young man, the observation punctuating her earlier thoughts. Her son had brought a young man home, and he was now a man himself. She had to swallow hard to keep too much emotion from brimming up. It was joy, most definitely, but tinged with mourning for days gone by. She looked from her husband's face to her son's, and the resemblance was even more astonishing than the last time she'd seen them together. They had the same broad smile, humor-filled eyes, and curly hair. Two of a kind.

"So, where are we bunking, Mom?" Tyler asked, already popping pieces of a muffin into his mouth.

"You two are out in the guest cottage," Stacey answered. "We thought you'd probably want a little privacy. I hate to run when you've just arrived, but Birdy needs to get to her swimming lesson. You boys can entertain yourselves for the afternoon?"

"Eighteen holes, remember?" Nathan responded with a nod to Tyler and Chase. "We'll stay out of trouble."

"I'm so glad you're home," Stacey said to Tyler as she pulled out her daughter's chair. "Come on, Birdy, let's shake a leg. When we get there, I'd like you to point out Jeffrey's mother for me."

THE CHILDREN shrieked as they splashed in the cool lake. Stacey looked up from under her large sun hat and Jackie O sunglasses and spotted Birdy in her bright pink bathing suit running away from a little boy. It appeared the class was playing tag.

"Doesn't look like swimming *lessons* to me," she muttered to herself, arranging her scrapbooking materials on the picnic table. A menagerie of paper-weighted family photos, stickers, paper frames, glue sticks, and scissors littered the workspace in front of her. She picked up the scissors and went to work, her mind playing its favorite game of a free-association stream of consciousness.

Just cut. And glue. Good thing the craft house had the acid-free glue this time. Photos can be ruined otherwise. To think I had to inform them! They're supposed to be the experts on these things. What is wrong with parents these days? Ten years old, and Birdy has already seen a penis. It's uncalled for. Disgusting. What kind of a mother lets her child run around showing their privates? I hope Birdy didn't touch it.... Where was the swimming teacher? I'll have to talk with him too.

Stacey picked up a photo of herself and Nathan from the previous Christmas. She examined her own joyful face beaming back and then grimaced as she looked at Nathan beside her, looking less than thrilled. With a few quick snips she cut out her own image and discarded the rest. Flipping through the holiday pile, she smiled as she found a photo of Nathan laughing. She traced the scissors around her husband and then glued both pictures onto a snowy background where the words "Happy Holidays" glittered above their heads.

There's a reason why people say "make memories." They don't just happen; you have to construct them. Satisfied with her work, she looked out toward the water. Birdy's swimming class was gathered in a circle around their coach, listening attentively. She scanned the little bodies for a bright pink bathing suit but found none. Searching the lake, she finally located Birdy standing a little ways off from her class with a boy her age. Stacey watched in horror as the boy pulled out the front of his shorts and their eyes went down. Her daughter's attention was intently fixated on the boy's bathing-suit region, or where his bathing suit should have been. *Jeffrey!*

Stacey stood, pulled off her sunglasses, and ran down to the water. "Birdy! Birdy! Get away from that boy!" Without waiting for her daughter to react, Stacey ran right into the lake, hiking her dress up around her hips. "Birdy! What are you doing? You two, come with me." Seeing no other option, Stacey let her dress fall into the water and grabbed a hand of each child, pulling them out of the lake.

"Mom! You're embarrassing me!" Birdy whined as she whipped her gaze to the swimming class and beach crowd.

"I'm embarrassing you? I wasn't the one cavorting out in the middle of the lake, in front of the whole beach." She turned to the boy. "I suppose you're Jeffrey?"

"I didn't do anysing!" he pleaded through his toothless kisser.

"I saw exactly what you did, you little pervert!" Stacey growled back.

"Excuse me? Is there a problem here?"

Stacey was too intent on not letting the little exhibitionist escape to take much notice of the woman who had approached them. "Yes, but I'll handle the situation."

"Well, I'd love to be a part of 'handling the situation.' This is my son," the woman informed Stacey, resting her hands on her bare hips.

Stacey took in the sight before her: a woman of about her age in a bright lime green bikini, jewelry dangling from her belly button. Her complete appraisal of the woman took less than two seconds. "Well, that makes sense. This little nudist son of yours has been showing my daughter his penis."

The woman bit her lip to try to suppress a growing smile.

"You think this is funny? It's a violation of her childhood!" Stacey reeled, anger at the injustice getting the better of her.

"I wasn't showing her my penis!" Jeffrey interrupted. "I wanted to show her a minnow!"

"Minnow. I'm sure." Stacey shook her head incredulously.

"Mom, he's telling the truth. He was just showing me a minnow he caught," Birdy testified on Jeffrey's behalf.

"This is unbelievable. I don't care what we all want to call it, children of ten should not be sharing that kind of thing."

Bikini Woman reached out and tousled her son's hair as if to forgive the whole incident. "Let's just relax. They're kids."

"At this rate, not for long!" Stacey shot back. Something cold and wet found its way into Stacey's hand. She looked down and flinched at the sight of a motionless, slimy little fish, which Jeffrey had pressed into her palm.

"See? I told you. I caught a minnow!" Jeffrey squealed, laughing uncontrollably at the reaction he'd gotten from Stacey and splashing around in the water. Bikini Woman just watched, amused.

"Birdy, grab your things. We're leaving." Stacey took Birdy by the arm again and marched her over to the picnic table. She began stuffing her scrapbooking supplies into a shoulder bag. "I think you've had enough swimming lessons. This afternoon we'll go to the community center and see what other activities they're offering."

"But Mom, I liked swimming."

Stacey planted her sunglasses on her face and led her daughter off the beach, careful to avoid the curious gazes she was sure were following her. "We can't always get what we'd like. We have to enjoy what we're given."

NATHAN COULDN'T help but smile when he caught the first glimpse of the Porsche as the garage door opened. It was a vintage convertible in mint green, a collector's dream. Nathan was a regular at auto shows, but just as an appreciator of classic cars. He'd never actually bought one before. This spring he'd begun going more regularly. He enjoyed the time away from the house on Saturday mornings mindlessly strolling between the cars. He'd never been a grease monkey, but he did appreciate the lines of a beautiful car and wasn't a stranger to the adrenaline rush achievable with a powerful engine. He enjoyed talking with the other men at the shows and had found an unspoken comradeship there. This was still a male-dominated zone, one that, if not completely understood, was at least tolerated by the women in their lives.

Eventually, the temptation to not only admire and touch one of the iron beauties on the show floor but to also own one became too great. He knew the cliché: he had recently had his thirty-sixth birthday, so maybe the purchase of a sports car was the official mile marker that middle age was upon him. The purchase was worth every cent. When he was in the driver's seat, he felt young again, in control of the future and the road ahead, and it seemed that life and its possibilities were limitless.

"A Porsche! Mint!" Tyler said. "Holy shit, do I get to inherit this?"

"Watch it. I'm not dead yet. So you like?" Nathan asked, watching Tyler and Chase excitedly taking in the car.

"Yeah, Dad. Sweet car," Tyler commented, jumping in the driver's seat. "I never thought you'd actually break down and buy one. I thought your Saturday morning excursions were just an excuse not to have to sit through Birdy's ballet classes."

"So who's up for eighteen holes?" Nathan asked, grabbing his golf clubs from a corner of the garage and tossing them in the trunk.

"Let's do it. Chase and I should stop by the pro shop to check in with Marty anyway. He'll probably want us to start working at the course tomorrow."

"You play golf, Chase?" Nathan asked, realizing that he didn't know a lot about Tyler's friend.

"Does Putt-Putt count?" Chase asked with a shrug.

"Prepare to get schooled," Tyler informed him with a shot to the ribs. "When's tee time?"

"About an hour," Nathan answered. "Why don't I show you guys the guest cottage? I finally got the shower installed."

"Nice work, Builder Bob," Tyler kidded. "Good timing on that too, not that I didn't love having to share a bathroom with Birdy since she rocketed onto the planet."

"Come on, smartass." Nathan laughed at his son's ribbing as he led the boys to the guest cottage. He and Tyler had always shared a sarcastic sense of humor, and Nathan prided himself on the fact that he had maintained the respected boundaries of a parent relationship while simultaneously enjoying a genuine friendship with his son. Of course, their relationship had grown from the unique beginning of Nathan stepping into fatherhood at the age of sixteen. He'd been a boy raising a boy in many ways. It certainly hadn't always been easy, and finishing high school with a baby posed a lot of challenges, but he and Stacey had made it work. When he looked at his son's face now, he couldn't imagine it happening any other way.

Tyler opened the door to the guest cottage and threw his bags on the floor. "Work in progress, huh?" he noted. Nathan watched him take in the unfinished ceiling and walls. Tyler was right, but nevertheless, it did have a certain charm to it. Two twin beds with matching nightstands and lamps split the room. A couple of surfboards, a pair of water skis, and a yellow go-cart rested against the far wall. An old library apothecary cabinet stood out on the opposite wall. Tyler walked over to it and paused to look up at Nathan before opening one of its drawers. "Still have all my football trading cards?"

Nathan nodded, smiling. "Yes, and still organized. Top row, Steelers, players from the six Super Bowl Championships, ascending years, left to right. Second to fourth rows, the players from the thirteen conference championship games, missing only—"

"—missing only tackle 'Mean' Joe Greene. I know, I know...," Tyler finished. Nathan recognized a trace of boyhood disappointment shadowing Tyler's face. He knew his son considered it a personal failure not to have completed his collection. Tyler's expression brightened as he noticed the shower Nathan had installed in the corner of the room. "Come on, Dad, that's hilarious. The bathroom isn't going to have walls?"

"It's open concept," Nathan defended himself.

"It's exhibitionist or lazy! My guess is you decided you'd rather spend your summer on the golf course than building practical things like walls for the guest cottage," Tyler said, walking over to the shower and trying a tap. "Well, at least it works."

"It's like loft living in the city. Walls are passé."

"Okay, Mr. Architect, maybe that line flies with your clients, but I know better. You were lazy."

Nathan shook his head. "I'll let you guys get changed. Remember, collared shirts for the club." Nathan closed the door behind him but paused at the sound of Chase's voice.

"I thought you said your dad was uptight."

"I don't know what's gotten into him. Must be a midlife crisis or something," Tyler answered.

So it is that obvious. Nathan shook his head.

"He still looks pretty young to me."

Well, thank you, Chase.

"I'm the product of teen pregnancy, remember? My parents had me when they were in high school." There was a pause and then an animated yell from Tyler. "Put some clothes on, man! Just because we're in the woods doesn't mean you have to go au naturel!"

The only reply was a *snap*.

"Owww! Lay off with the towel!" Chase yelled back. "Gross! Get your disgusting pit stains away from me!"

Nathan smiled to himself and walked toward the house. *Boys will be boys....*

A SMALL crowd was enjoying their postgame drinks on the patio of the Prospect Lake Clubhouse, overlooking the first tee. Nathan selected a driver and took a few practice swings before toeing up to the ball. "Relax, breathe, and don't kill it," he reminded himself on his backswing. Following through, he anticipated the shot and looked up the fairway a millisecond before connecting. The ball sailed a hundred and fifty yards straight ahead and then abruptly sliced to the left, landing on the opposing fairway.

"You looked up," Tyler informed him, already planting his tee into the soil.

"Yeah, I know." Nathan stood back and observed as his son took a few practice swings and coached Chase on his skills. One thing was certain: Tyler wasn't lacking in the confidence department.

"Gotta keep your eye on the ball, Chase. Visualize where you want the ball to go. Just like sex. Get it in the hole." Tyler paused for a rare second of silence before connecting with the ball and sending it flying. "Just like that. All right, Chase, you're up."

Chase couldn't have looked any less thrilled to be there. It made sense: not only was it his first time golfing, but he had to tee off with a crowd watching from the patio. Nothing like trial by fire. Nathan watched as he picked through the clubs in his rental bag and finally selected a driver, no doubt trying to match it to what he'd seen Tyler and himself use. As Chase set his ball on the tee, Tyler nattered in his ear.

"Okay, this part is like foreplay. You have to work up to actually getting it in the cup. If you can get a hole in one, all the better. But most guys have to do it in a few stages. What you wanna do is cut down on those stages and just pop it in there as soon as you can, but be careful not to overshoot."

"I thought golf was a quiet game." Chase shot him a look over his shoulder before giving a hard practice swing.

"You gotta relax. You'll overshoot. Nice and easy now," Tyler coached.

"Tyler, knock it off. Just let the guy play," Nathan cut in, using his fatherly voice.

Chase looked up and gave Nathan a little smile—an acknowledgment and a thank-you.

Nathan couldn't help but smile back before giving him a nod to go at his own pace.

Chase pulled the club back like a baseball bat and all but attacked the ground with his swing. He did, however, make contact, and the ball flew about thirty feet across the lawn and landed directly in a sand trap.

"Good. That's…." Nathan struggled for a moment. "Well, you connected, that's… good."

"Now I'd call that shooting blanks. You gotta visualize the cup, man. Visualize the cup," Tyler chimed in as they picked up their golf bags and headed down the first fairway. "Just think of me like your own motivational speaker. You should have me coach you in sex. If I did, you'd probably get some. It'd improve your golf game too."

"Tyler!" The threesome turned to see a raven-haired vixen decked out in a white sun visor, golf skirt, and polo waving from the clubhouse patio.

"As I was saying, actions speak louder than words, and that is trouble in a short skirt. I'll catch up with you guys," Tyler said as he did an about-face and jogged back up to the clubhouse.

Nathan read the question on Chase's face and tried to fill in the blanks. "That's Bre, Tyler's on-again, off-again summer girlfriend. He didn't mention her?"

"No... but he might have. I start to get confused just with the girls at college. I think he has a different girlfriend for every class he takes," Chase said, still watching as Tyler planted a big kiss on Bre, as if last summer were only yesterday.

"I can't imagine what having Tyler as your roommate would be like." Nathan laughed.

Chase picked up his golf bag again and started to walk toward the sand trap and his ball. "He's not a chip off the old block?"

"Well, not quite in that way. Other ways, yeah. I mean, we have a lot in common. I never had the opportunity to be young and restless in college. I was already trying to be a grown-up—" Nathan stopped himself. He hadn't even thought about that time for so long. It was something that had developed into an unspoken understanding in the house: their lives had started when he had been offered the job at the architecture firm, when they began to make enough money to live comfortably, when he and Stacey finally began to appear old enough to be parents. Anything before that wasn't talked about. The past was the past; it didn't really have relevance today.

Nathan watched as Chase stepped into the sand trap and again began to rummage through his bag. He looked like a lost puppy. "Find the one labelled with an SW—it's a sand wedge. Easy to remember, right?"

Chase looked up and smiled gratefully. The kid had a grin that was contagious, Nathan considered as he felt one creeping across his own face. He set down his own golf bag on the sand trap's bank and stepped in to give some pointers. "Let's see your swing. Remember, don't lift your head too soon." As soon as the words escaped his mouth, Nathan grimaced. "Jeez, I'm sorry. Like father, like son, huh?"

Chase smirked at him and then gave a home-run-worthy baseball swing. "I'll take pointers."

"Okay, you've got passion behind it, that's good. Let's just focus some of that energy." Nathan knelt down, and after taking the club from Chase, laid it down perpendicular to his toes. "Use your club to make sure you're pointed in the right direction. Feet shoulder-width apart."

Nathan stood and walked around behind Chase, pushing the backs of his knees, buckling them momentarily. "Slight bend in the knees. Not quite that much. Look where you want the ball to go. Put your head down and lift with the club. Now I'm gonna cross the tree line to my goddamn ball."

Nathan climbed out of the sand trap, picked up his bag, and started hiking up the fairway, watching for his ball, but his mind was on anything but golf. He'd been catapulted back to his teenage years, as confusing and brief as they were. When you had to start changing diapers by your seventeenth birthday, it kind of stunted the exploration of the joys of sex.

He didn't resent Stacey for the pregnancy. They had been young, and they'd both wanted to experiment. He'd had no idea how those few early explorations would alter his destiny so drastically. He considered what it must be like for Tyler at college, living a life that in some ways might have been similar to his own had that not happened: carefree, sexually liberated, spontaneous. He instinctively switched back into parent mode, hoping that Tyler was always safe and used protection. He'd had the discussion with Tyler often enough he was sure his son had taken it to heart. It was a difficult discussion to have with his own "miracle" baby, to simultaneously express gratitude for having Tyler in his life and caution him against the difficulties of becoming a parent too young.

Everyone was different, though. Chase was the same age as Tyler and didn't seem to be as sex obsessed, or maybe he was and Nathan hadn't witnessed it yet. Most college guys were. A healthy obsession with sex.... He laughed at the idea. He'd spent so long trying to repress sexual thoughts and feelings and just seem normal. And he'd succeeded. He and Stacey had one boy and one girl, and in every way theirs appeared to be a perfectly constructed family.

Smack!

Nathan jumped at the sound more than from the impact of a golf ball hitting his bag. He turned to see Tyler and Chase running down the fairway from the sand trap.

"Fore!" Chase yelled.

"Yeah, it's a little late for that," Nathan called back. "What are you doing? Trying to kill me?"

"I'm so sorry! I didn't mean to," Chase stammered, red-faced from the run and embarrassment as he reached Nathan.

Nathan couldn't help but smile. "It's okay. No harm done. You just learned two things about golf. Number one, my fault. Never walk ahead of another player, even if you think they can't hit the ball more than thirty feet. And number two, keep your eye on the ball. You're likely to hit toward whatever you're looking at."

Chase lowered his eyes, suddenly seeming to have a keen interest in the grass as Tyler caught up. "You know, this isn't dodgeball, Chase. We're not trying to hit other players. Golf is a game of patience. I'm here for you. I'm not here for me."

"Shut up," Nathan and Chase said in unison and then looked at each other and laughed.

"Jinx. You know what that means? You owe me a beer after the game," Chase teased Nathan.

"I owe you a beer? You're the one who nearly killed me!"

"Gentlemen," Tyler said as he stepped between them, "I have a feeling there could be quite a tally by the time this game is over. May I remind you we haven't even reached the first green? Which I'm probably on, with my first shot," Tyler bragged, walking ahead. "I'm voting the loser buys today. So, Chase, we can just ask Marty to take that off your future paychecks, and Dad, as you know, I do take direct deposit into my bank account."

NATHAN CLOSED his eyes and tipped his head back, enjoying the warm water rushing over his face. The shower was a welcome sanctuary after the golf game. It hadn't been his best: he had shot a whopping fifteen over par. He would have stopped keeping score early on if it hadn't been for Tyler gloating every time he got to bring out the little pencil and scorecard to tally the strokes. Truth was, his mind had been far from the game. There was a strange feeling in his chest that he couldn't quite place, almost a nervous excitement. Anxiety, maybe? It was his first week of vacation. He was probably just winding down from the stress of the office. Without the minutiae of work weighing him down, he was relishing the opportunity for his mind to wander.

Chase was an artist—he'd learned that much on the golf course. Well, he definitely wasn't a golfer; that had become pretty apparent. Nathan imagined Chase working late on a canvas in a studio. The image blurred to one of himself seated at a drafting table in his office working late on plans for a new restaurant. *An artist, most likely a lone wolf.* That could explain the lack of discussion about girlfriends. He was definitely handsome enough. That odd sensation crept back up into his gut, pulling at him from the inside. He took several deep breaths to quell the sensation, then turned off the shower and shook the excess water from his hair.

As he dried and dressed, Nathan found himself looking in the mirror. No, not just looking, but really observing. Like he was an outsider watching this person go through the routine of readying himself. He found it disturbing. He didn't know who that person was. The whole manner was so procedural, orchestrated, and anything but spontaneous. When had he become the man staring back at him?

"You're thirty-six," he whispered to the reflection, looking it deep in the eyes. "Crow's-feet, laugh lines, widow's peak... it's all you. You've earned it all."

Nathan had always kept himself in good shape. He hit the gym, he played squash a couple of mornings every week in town, and he ran. The other guys at the office thought he was obsessive. That was hardly it. He'd just never wanted to become his father. He'd seen him suffer the unnecessary pain and hospital time of two heart attacks. Genetics might have had something to do with it, but it had been his father's horrible grasp of fundamental nutrition and lack of exercise that had really done him in. Nathan had no intention of following in those footsteps. He also recognized that already his body wasn't what it used to be. It seemed he had to run farther, lift heavier, and exercise longer just to maintain his body every year.

After pulling on a shirt, he buttoned top to bottom and then began unbuttoning again when he looked in the mirror. Too stuffy. He walked to his dresser and flipped through a stack of folded T-shirts, selecting a heather gray one. After pulling it on, he walked back to the mirror and nodded, noting the slight stretch over his chest and biceps.

Nathan walked into the living room and paused when he saw Chase staring at a family portrait on the wall. He seemed deep in thought, like he was in the middle of a complicated equation. Nathan cleared his throat and then joined Chase in front of the portrait. "Sight for sore eyes, huh? Your family do them too?"

"No, haven't in a while," Chase answered without taking his gaze off the wall.

"I'd really rather hang art there, but Stacey insists. Maybe one day we'll have one of your pieces. I'd love to see some of your work."

"I sold everything I had left at college. Coffeehouses, a few little galleries and stuff. No big deal. Good way to make some pocket change, right?"

"Well, if you're selling all your work, you must be pretty decent."

"Half-decent," Chase corrected.

"So what do you paint? Landscapes and stuff?"

Chase turned from the family portrait. "No, people are more interesting to me." He smiled that half smile again, somewhere between shy and mischievous, before his attention turned to an open box of photos on a credenza. "Is it all right if I look through these?"

Nathan caught himself with that anxious feeling in his gut again and forced his mind to operate rationally. "That's what they're for." He picked up a stack of the photos and began flipping through to distract himself. "This is us together in Boston. Stacey and me, so it would have been right after the wedding."

"You got married right after high school, huh?" Chase said, taking the photo from Nathan to examine.

"That's right."

"Why'd you move to Boston?" Chase asked, looking up from the corner of his eyes.

"School of Design at Harvard, History of Art and Architecture with a focus on… building stuff." Nathan swallowed the words, ridiculously conscious of the sound of his own voice. Why did Chase care? *He's a guest, just making polite conversation.*

"Here's one of Tyler. I didn't know he played football," Chase said, sounding surprised, and handed the photo to Nathan.

Nathan smiled at the confusion as he peered at himself in his old Crimson jersey. "That's not Tyler, that's me. I haven't looked at this stuff in years."

"You haven't changed much." Nathan's chest swelled at Chase's compliment. "Were you on scholarship?"

"It's how I got through college. I couldn't have done it otherwise, not with Stacey and Tyler. Barely made it as it was," Nathan confided.

"Me too. I was lucky to get a full ride. There's no way I'd be at that school otherwise," Chase admitted. "Wow, architect, football team—you must have been the big man on campus."

"He was." Nathan and Chase whirled around to see Stacey crossing toward them. "I had to show up to all the games to remind the cheerleaders he was a married man." Stacey slipped an arm around Nathan and gave him a squeeze. "Oh, I really need to pop those in an album. Dinner's ready, boys."

Nathan and Chase followed Stacey into the dining room, where Tyler and Birdy were already seated at the table. As they settled into their seats, Nathan surveyed the banquet his wife had prepared, which included a large turkey with all the trimmings. "That's why the house is so hot. You cooked a turkey in June?"

Ignoring the sarcasm, Stacey stood and began serving, "It's our first meal as a whole family again. I thought it was more appropriate than throwing burgers on the barbecue."

"I like burgers better," Birdy chimed in, poking at the mashed potatoes on her plate.

"Remember how we talked about enjoying what we're given? We can have burgers another night." Stacey dished out another plate and handed it to Tyler. "How was the golf game?"

"Chase is gonna need some more coaching, but he pulled through okay for his first time out," Tyler said, opting for fingers over fork to pop a piece of turkey in his mouth.

"Tell the truth, Tyler. We beat you," Nathan said.

"Because I gave you both, like, fifty mulligans!"

Birdy looked up from creating a swimming pool of gravy in her mashed potatoes. "What's a mulligan?"

"Golf talk, honey. Eat your turkey," Stacey instructed, finally sitting with her own plate across from Nathan at the head of the table.

"We hardly even saw Dad. He was playing his usual game, up the opposite fairway," Tyler said between mouthfuls, still seemingly unaware that utensils lay on either side of his plate.

"Your father does tend to go about things backwards," Stacey commented as she stabbed a baby carrot with her fork, gaze fixed on her plate.

"What's that supposed to mean?" Nathan looked up, ready for a battle if one was threatening.

"Nothing. It was a joke, dear." Stacey pushed her food around on her plate before turning to Chase. "So, Chase, what do your parents do?"

Chase put down his fork, looking surprised to be suddenly injected into the conversation. "Well, Mom doesn't work…."

"A stay-at-home mom like me! No wonder you've turned out to be such a respectable young man." Stacey beamed, apparently validated for her own choices in life by a woman she'd never met.

"Actually, she's nothing like you. She doesn't work because… I don't really know why. Not because she was ever busy being a mom."

Nathan tried to shoot Stacey a "stop while you're ahead" look, but she missed it and plowed forward in her innocent questioning. "So, your father works?"

Chase shook his head and took another bite. "He died when I was five. May I have some more potatoes?"

Stacey jumped up and began dishing out more food. "By all means, let me help. Oh! I almost forgot!"

Nathan sat watching his wife in disbelief as she busied herself lighting the candles on the table. His family continued with dinner, all awkwardly ignoring the fact that their guest had just revealed some upsetting aspects of his past. That was how the Davidson family functioned. They didn't speak about things that made them feel uncomfortable. If anything unpleasant arose, they tried to rush past it by filling the moment with so much minutiae that an authentic feeling had no space to take root. He looked at Chase, now animatedly talking and laughing with Tyler. Nathan had a feeling their guest had become a master at disguising reality himself.

CHASE STARED into the fire, trying to locate the whitish blue flames, the concentration of the most intense heat. The fire licked at the pile of logs dug into the beach, and Chase watched, mesmerized. What was it about fire that had fascinated men since the dawn of time? It was hypnotic as it destroyed what it was given and simultaneously gave the gift of heat and light. What was also hypnotic was the soliloquy spewing forth from the girl sitting on the log beside him. He could feel her gaze blasting him from the right. She was obviously not as enraptured by the fire. Maybe soliloquy was the wrong word, Chase thought, because she wasn't just speaking to herself, although she might as well have been. He pondered that for a moment. If a monologue isn't heard or acknowledged by its intended audience, is it then in fact a soliloquy? He thought he could justify that rationale. But then again, he was occasionally grunting an acknowledgment, so that would be acknowledging her, so maybe it was more like a really long monologue. The truth was he had no idea what she had been saying, and as he glanced over at her he felt a twinge of compassion for the girl. It was obvious now that they had been set up, and she was giving it all she had.

Christie was a pretty Asian girl and a biochemistry major or something like that. Chase had only registered the first two pieces of information Tyler had told him as they drove to the beach so he could identify the girl he was supposed to spend the evening with. It wasn't like this was the first time Tyler had set him up; it was a regular occurrence. He always enthusiastically thanked Tyler for his efforts and then fell into a melancholy of anxiety for the rest of the evening. And so now here they all were, in another night of courteous discomfort, his own little personal hell. Chase sat staring into the fire, wishing to be absorbed by its heat and taken away from this situation. His date was overexerting herself in a vain attempt to gain his interest and make it a successful evening. Tyler and Bre were obviously "on again" as they cuddled on the opposite side of the fire.

Chase watched the newly reacquainted couple through the dancing orange flames and felt heat climbing up his neck and onto his cheeks. He decided not to torture himself by deciphering whether it was being caused by the fire or by jealousy. *If* it was jealousy, it wasn't directed at either one of them in particular, just a twisting in his gut, a tightening of the muscles there. It wasn't that he wanted Bre, or even the more likely possibility that he might actually want Tyler. Even if that was the case, he couldn't allow that thought to reside in his consciousness for too long. If it took root, he feared it would cause him even more restless confusion than he already suffered. He couldn't quite put his finger on it, but he realized he harbored some resentment toward Tyler. It just didn't seem fair. Tyler had been born into a practically perfect family, was handsome and charismatic, could obviously have his choice of careers and women, and was straight. How much easier could life get? It was a strange brew that stirred inside Chase as he watched his best friend, and he suddenly realized through the murky jealousy and resentment that he didn't in fact want Tyler, as he'd feared. It was more than that: he wanted to be him.

He wanted the power to make people fall in love with him. He wanted to be regarded as confident and cool. He wanted to feel comfortable in his own skin and not worry about what other people thought about him. He wanted to stop being the yes-man always looking to Tyler for approval. He wanted to stop pretending to be something he wasn't. And he wanted to stop being set up on these stupid dates.

"And then right when the fireworks started, he asked her to marry him!" Christie exclaimed, beaming from the excitement of her own story.

Chase turned to her to see if this was a pause in her monologue or the end of it. It appeared as if she was finished, and so he felt compelled to offer an insightful response: "Wow."

"I know right? So romantic. Growing up is so weird. I'm going to three weddings this summer." Christie turned and said this loud enough for the whole group to hear, her gaze landing on Bre and Tyler suspiciously.

"Don't expect an invitation from me anytime soon."

Chase looked up to see that a handsome black guy had walked up to the fire, a case of beer under his arm.

"You need to find a girl willing to wake up to your ugly mug every morning first," Tyler joked as he stood to give the new guy a hug.

"Who needs one girl when I can have a whole cheerleading squad?"

The guy laughed, sitting down on the log beside Chase, opening the twelve-pack and tossing one to Tyler and one to Bre. "You almost done with that sports medicine degree? Ready to be my masseuse when I get drafted to the NFL?"

"When you make the draft, give me a call," Tyler promised, laughing.

"Beer?" The guy had turned to Chase, his hand extended with a bottle and his big brown eyes dancing like there was a joke forming in his head.

"Yeah, sure," Chase replied, taking notice of the muscles stretching the cotton of the new guy's T-shirt.

"Jarod, this is Chase. Chase, Jarod," Christie offered, snuggling into Chase's shoulder as if it was actually necessary to get that close to make the introduction. "Chase is a painter."

"No shit. I did that for a few summers with a cousin," Jarod said, twisting the cap off his beer.

"Not houses, silly. Chase paints on canvas. He's an artist," Christie explained, taking obvious pride in her date's talents. "It's totally different."

"Well, you get dirty doing either one. I just use a smaller brush," Chase offered.

"You're funny. And cute," Christie said, leaning even further into Chase's shoulder, if that were possible. "If you ever need a model...."

"I'm more of a landscape guy." Chase thought he saw Jarod chuckle as he took a pull of his beer. The conversation with Christie subsided for a while, allowing Chase to go back to obsessing without interruption. A light breeze drifted off the lake and swirled through the flames, causing them to snap deliciously around the wood. Looking up the beach, he could see clusters of other people gathered around beach fires. Huddled close, enjoying the warmth of the fire and each other. Chase felt a tap against his shoe and looked down to see a blue sneaker resting against his own white one. He glanced up at Jarod, who stared straight into the fire as he spoke.

"You watch football?"

"Yeah, sure," Chase lied. Did it count if Tyler was watching a game in their dorm room while he read a book?

Jarod looked over at him with a smile. "Who's your team?"

"Ummm.... Steelers?" Chase answered.

Jarod just nodded, the smile spreading farther across his face. "Oh yeah? Who's your favorite player?"

"Uh, I don't know, man." Chase silently cursed himself for not paying attention during at least one game. Jarod's knee brushed against his own, just for a second, and then rested there, a millimeter away. The sensation sent an electric current through Chase, up from the base of his spine, into his throat, and back again. He could feel it shooting between them as the tiny hairs on their legs danced against each other, barely touching but sending that roller coaster up through his stomach each time they did.

On Chase's right side, Christie still hung on his shoulder, feeling for all the world like a dead weight and one he'd do anything to get out from under. On his left side, Jarod continued to sit looking into the fire, drinking his beer and letting his leg accidentally touch him for all too fleeting moments. His left side was zinging with energy and his right felt unnecessarily burdened. He almost laughed at the absurdity but caught himself.

Jarod suddenly turned and chuckled. "Too much beer, I gotta take a leak."

Chase's left side cooled as Jarod left, his gaze following him up into the tree line. Unfortunately it was clear that Christie saw this as an opportunity to make a move again, and she began a mini-interrogation. "So you and Tyler are going to be working at the golf course?"

"Yup." Chase took a swig of his beer and stared across the flames at Tyler and Bre, who were fully engaged in an Olympic-level game of tonsil hockey.

"So you're going to be here for the whole summer, then?"

"That's the plan."

"We should hang out," Christie suggested, anything but casual.

"Yeah, sure."

Christie noticed Chase eyeing Tyler and Bre across the fire and lowered her voice conspiratorially. "They're ridiculously cute, right? Every summer, back together, just like clockwork."

"They're right on schedule," Chase offered.

"Maybe we could go out with Bre and Tyler sometime, you know like a—"

"Will you excuse me for a second... too much beer...," Chase interrupted and stood without waiting for an answer. The last thing he wanted to hear coming out of her mouth was the word date. It would just make it that much more complicated, with higher expectations and more deceit on his part. He'd gotten pretty good at using his dedication to scholarly pursuits as an excuse at university, but that wasn't going to fly here. He needed time to think up a valid reason for why a summer romance wasn't on his schedule.

Chase's eyes adjusted to the darkness away from the fire as he made his way up the beach to the tree line where he'd seen Jarod enter the forest. He wasn't even really sure what he was doing. Maybe it was an instance of thinking with his little head instead of his big one. At least when he was letting his pelvis lead the way, it prevented him from considering consequences, repercussions, and reality, which all seemed to hit him over the head simultaneously as he entered the woods.

What the hell was he thinking? He was going to march up here and confront Jarod and say… what exactly? That he thought possibly there was some chemistry down at the fire when their legs accidentally brushed against each other? This was a bad idea, bad idea, bad idea. He was about to turn around and walk right out of the woods when he saw Jarod casually leaning against a tree, twirling a couple rocks in his hand like Baoding balls and watching him.

"Hey." Jarod exhaled coolly without moving, his eyes still locked on Chase.

"Hey. I just came to uh…," Chase stammered, not having the faintest idea how to finish that sentence.

"That's cool, go ahead," Jarod said, still twirling the rocks between his fingers.

Take a leak. That's right, that's all I came up here to do. Chase slowly turned and unzipped, imagining Jarod's gaze scrutinizing his movements. His head felt light and buoyant, both the big one and the little one, and the last thing he had motor control over was aiming down right now. "Actually, I uh… I don't really have to." Chase adjusted his erection, zipped up, and turned back slowly, trying to laugh it off.

"Me neither." Jarod dropped the rocks and walked toward Chase. Chase turned and started to head out of the woods, but he felt a hand on his shoulder. "Going so soon?"

A strong arm encircled his waist and skillfully turned him back around. They stood like that for what seemed an eternity, hips pressed together, faces inches apart, sharing the air between them. Chase's breath came in rapid, shallow bites. He could smell Jarod's cologne mixed faintly with the clean smell of detergent. The current of energy ran on an accelerating loop from his groin to the top of his head and back again, over and over, faster and faster as Jarod pressed harder against him. "Jarod, what are you doing?"

"Come on, let's have a little fun."

"What do you mean?" Chase managed between his shallow breaths.

"You know what I mean," Jarod replied, his chocolate eyes imploring him.

"I can't...," Chase said, not entirely sure why his mouth was contradicting every other part of his body.

"Yes, you can," Jarod insisted, leaning in to kiss Chase, his hands pulling Chase even harder against himself.

And Chase's body yelled back yes. He had never felt so completely free, so completely right about something he had long ago decided was completely wrong. His skin tingled all over as his tongue pressed against Jarod's in a ferocious duel. The cool night air rushed into his lungs, and he tasted cedar trees, faint campfire smoke, and the damp moss clinging to the trees and rocks around them. In a single isolated moment, he heard the waves lazily lapping up against the beach, their friends laughing around the campfire, and the hum of the stars high above them. He thrilled at the feeling of the lips brushing against his and the contented growl that rumbled through Jarod's chest and reverberated in his own. This was being alive—this knowing, this awareness.

Snap!

Chase instinctively pulled away and spun around, looking for the source of the sound. "Did you hear that?"

"It's nothing, come on," Jarod encouraged, grabbing Chase by the belt buckle and pulling him back into another kiss.

"I can't, I'm not...," Chase began.

"Gay?"

"No, I am, it's just...." Chase didn't finish the sentence. He'd come out for the first time and it had just happened, no big premeditated delivery, just simple and true.

"Not out? Me either, it's okay," Jarod confessed. They looked at each other and smiled conspiratorially, both inexperienced players in the game of coming out. "We should get back. Hold on. What are you doing tomorrow night?"

"Trying to not have a date with Christie." Chase laughed. "I don't know. I'll probably be with Tyler."

"Don't tell him, okay? If he knew about me, he'd freak out," Jarod cautioned, reaching out and giving Chase's hand a squeeze. "Let's go."

Chase considered Jarod's words as they headed back across the beach to the campfire. Would Tyler really freak out if he knew about Jarod? If that was true, what would he do if he found out about Chase? He decided maybe it was best if his newfound honesty with himself stayed hidden a little while longer, at least until he'd had time to reflect on it. As they reached the campfire, Tyler was covering it with buckets of sand, and Christie and Bre were folding up the blankets and putting empty beer bottles into cases.

"Hey guys, we're packing it in," Tyler said, pouring another bucket of sand over the ashes. "Chase, can you drive? We gotta take Bre home and I'm a little buzzed."

"He's a lot buzzed," Bre corrected.

"So that's a night, huh?" Jarod asked casually, picking up a few empty bottles. "When did we get so old? Christie, I can give you a ride home if you want."

"Thanks, Jarod." Christie turned to Chase and slipped a paper in his pocket, planting a quick kiss on his cheek. "Give me a call sometime."

"Hey, where's my kiss?" Jarod walked up to Christie, arms wide to receive a hug. "You're laying all your love on the new guy. How about some sugar for us old friends?"

After watching Christie fulfill Jarod's request, Chase walked over and extended his hand to shake.

"Ah, come on in for the real thing." Jarod pulled him into a hug and whispered in his ear. "Not a word, got it?"

"Yeah." Chase swallowed, already feeling mixed up about their stolen moments in the woods.

Jarod pulled away and punched Chase in the arm. "Steelers! Ha! Your team is going down, buddy." He draped an arm around Christie, and they headed for his truck. Chase swallowed hard as he watched them go.

CHASE QUICKLY made his way through the Beemer's gears into fifth and sped down the twisty lake road. He knew he was headed the right way from Tyler's vague directions; he didn't know exactly how to get where he was going, but he wasn't worried. It was a lake, hence some kind of closed loop, and Bre's family's summer house was somewhere on the water. Head in either direction on the lake road, and he'd eventually find it.

His mind, which had been so clear and free in those fleeting moments with Jarod in the woods, was now back to its incessant rambling. He'd felt so courageous when it was just the two of them there, like whatever anyone else thought didn't matter and couldn't touch him. *You were hiding in the woods under the veil of darkness,* he wryly reminded himself. *That's not all that courageous.* But even still, he'd taken a first step. He'd followed his instincts, and they were correct. He'd sensed that Jarod was interested in doing more than just talking football with him, and he'd been right. What would happen if he followed his instincts even more closely? Could he free himself from his own mind and its constant chatter and inhibitions?

He got excited again as he imagined Jarod's mouth on his own, as he felt the phantom pressure of the other boy's muscled body pressed against him. One thing was certain: the summer was lining up to be a lot more exciting. He glanced in the rearview mirror and was surprised to find himself smiling as he saw Tyler and Bre making out like cats in heat. He understood now that they were just following their instincts, lost in their own special world. And every time Tyler had tried to set Chase up on a date, it was because he cared. He wanted Chase to feel what he had felt tonight. Chase realized he cared for Tyler even more now that he understood the motivation behind all those setups, which he'd found annoying in the past. Tyler was doing it because he cared about Chase. He was just unfortunately misguided, through no fault of his own.

His mind flickered back to what Jarod had said. Would Tyler really freak out if he knew? Had something happened in the past to give Jarod that insight, or was he just projecting his own fear about the situation? In Chase's opinion Tyler had always been nice to everyone, the type of guy who easily blended with all the different cliques at college, but then they'd never really hung out with anyone who was gay before. He couldn't even recall a time when the subject of gay people had come up. Maybe Jarod was right. Maybe Tyler would freak out.

"This is it. Turn right into that next driveway." Tyler emerged from the back, wrapping an arm around each front seat to give directions. Chase pulled into the long tree-lined driveway and up to a beautiful A-frame log cabin. He watched in the mirror as the lovers shared another long kiss goodnight.

"It's nice to be back. Together, I mean," Bre said, opening her door.

"Yeah."

"You'll call me tomorrow, right?"

"Yes, I'll call you tomorrow," Tyler said, climbing out of the backseat after her and giving her one last kiss before jumping in the passenger seat. "Fun night, huh?"

Chase put the car in reverse and backed up to the lake road. "Yeah, fun night. So, you and Bre are back together, huh? Just like that."

"Just like that."

"Is it serious this time?"

"Nah. I mean, yeah, serious for a summer fling. I don't know." Tyler laughed, pulling the passenger-seat mirror down to check his mug. "Man, my lips are raw. She was eating me alive!"

"So you're not in love with her?" Chase asked, throwing the stick shift into first gear as he pulled onto the lake road.

"She smells better than you if that's what you're asking. What is this? Like twenty questions?" Tyler joked, flipping the mirror back up.

"Just wondering."

"I think Christie's into you." Tyler offered the obvious.

"Yeah, she told me."

"So? What are you gonna do about it?" Tyler asked, clearly excited that his matchmaking might have actually found a match. "I think Jarod's into Christie too. I'd move fast if I were you."

Though wary of how Tyler might react, Chase was nevertheless tempted to admit he had a sneaking suspicion that Jarod was interested in someone else. He wanted to tell him so badly, wanted to share the amazing experience he'd had in the woods, to tell Tyler he finally understood what it was like to be excited about someone. That was what best friends did, wasn't it? Share everything: no secrets, no shame. But then he thought of Jarod and realized he also had a new friend who he owed something to. He owed it to Jarod to keep his mouth shut, at least for now. "I move at my own pace."

"Yeah, first gear," Tyler joked.

Chase rolled his eyes and shared the laugh as he accelerated and shifted the car up through the gears. Maybe it was time he accelerated his love life too….

NATHAN TRIED desperately to focus on the board game as Birdy drew another question card from the deck. They were playing boys against girls with him, Tyler, and Chase forming a team against Stacey and Birdy. The game was called Identity Crisis?, and the congruity between this and his current frame of mind wasn't lost on him. The admission of his mounting midlife crisis was beginning to feel inevitable. He'd been greeted by crisis before, and he always made quick, rational decisions and moved forward. He wasn't one to dwell on the potential paradoxes of a problem. So what the hell was the matter with him lately? He couldn't seem to get off the hamster wheel of self-doubt and second-guessing. Each question only led to more questions, and he was creating a whole series of "what if" scenarios, an elaborate "choose your own adventure" novel of roads not taken. That was part of what was currently missing in his life, any sense of adventure. His existence had become rote, mechanical, and the most abhorrent adjective he could imagine—predictable.

It wasn't a feeling of not having accomplished anything. He was quite proud, in a quiet way, of his family, his success at the architecture firm, and his ability to afford a lifestyle he considered very comfortable. But what now? He had worked so diligently on pushing the boulder up the hill for the past twenty years. It felt like the challenge was over now. Was the only excitement left to push the boulder down the other side and follow it down, turning over and over, day after day in the same monotonous fashion until one day everything just… stopped? He shuddered at the thought.

"Daddy? Daddy! It's your turn." Birdy caught his attention by waving her hand in front of his face, each finger capped with a game piece like thimbles.

"Time's up, Little Miss Muffet." Stacey saved him by beginning to pack up the game. "I said we could play until eight o'clock, and it's eight fifteen. Time for you to have your bath."

"But Mom!" Birdy complained.

"No buts, just your butt in the tub," Nathan said with a wink.

"Good night, boys," Stacey said as she took the game in one hand and Birdy's hand in the other and headed for the bathroom.

Tyler looked up at Chase from another text message on his phone, a distraction that had kept him half-attentive all evening. "I'm gonna take the girls to a movie. You want to come?"

"Nah, I'm good here, man, thanks. I'm pretty swacked. I think I'll call it an early night."

"All right, suit yourself. Playing hard to get, are we?" Tyler asked, already on his way out. Chase shrugged.

"Christie will be disappointed," Nathan said. "Already have a girlfriend?"

"No, but I… I already know I'm not into it, so why pretend and then let her down?"

"Quite the player, are you?" Nathan laughed.

"I didn't mean it like that. Our interests are just a little too similar." Chase focused his attention out the window.

"You want another beer?" Nathan asked, getting out of his seat and heading to the kitchen. "Come on, let me show you the best place in the house."

Before turning into the kitchen, Nathan saw Chase raise his eyebrows curiously and get up to follow. Nathan noticed that for the first time all evening his mind was refreshingly quiet and clear.

THE BEST place in the house was not in the house at all. It was on top of the house. Nathan noticed Chase's eyebrows arch even higher as he leaned a ladder against the house and climbed up, his beer bottle stuffed in the back pocket of his jeans so he could have a two-handed grip. Nathan turned and held the ladder in place when he reached the top and waved down to Chase. "Come on up!"

He smiled, watching Chase place his own beer in a back pocket and make his way up the ladder. Nathan reached out and gave Chase a hand when he reached the top rung, and then for a second almost let go; there was a warmth there he hadn't expected.

This was Nathan's favorite place in the house, one he'd only shared with Tyler previously. The roof had a very gentle slope, and Nathan crossed it to where two lawn chairs lay covered with fallen pine needles and leaves. He shook them off and unfolded the chairs to face the lake far below. Chase settled into the seat beside him and pulled the cap off his beer. The summer sun was just beginning to set, and the sky was a brilliant tie-dye of orange, red, and mauve.

"Makes you feel kinda small, doesn't it?" Nathan finally asked, interrupting the quiet between them.

"Yeah. I guess if we only get to live once, you want to make sure you're doing the things you want. It goes by so fast."

Nathan couldn't help but laugh. "You have no idea."

Chase continued, obviously lost in his own thoughts. "I guess I just want to leave my mark somehow, make a difference...."

"Like with your painting?"

"Maybe, I don't know."

"Well, what would you want to change?" Nathan asked.

"I don't know. Just stuff," Chase answered, his gaze locked on the lake.

"Sounds like some heavy... stuff," Nathan said and then allowed another silence to pass between them.

"I guess I've just been thinking about, well, what are you supposed to do if you like someone and there's a possibility it could upset someone else?"

"Why would it upset the other person?"

"Well, maybe the other person always imagined you with someone else and so they'd be disappointed. But maybe it's not worth risking their disappointment because what if the person you like isn't even who you're supposed to be with in the end?" Chase asked, only occasionally looking at Nathan out of the corner of his eye.

"Is this about Christie?"

"No! That would make it so much... easier." Chase shook his head, an ironic grin shaping his mouth. They fell into a silence again. Nathan wasn't sure which questions to ask and could only guess at what the problem might be. The sky had given up its bright orange hues and was dressed in the light purples of twilight when Chase finally spoke again. "Was it weird getting married right out of high school?"

Nathan was taken aback by the new focus of the conversation. "I don't know about weird. It's just what happened."

"So you never dated anyone else, then?"

Nathan shook his head. "We were planning on going to different colleges, but then... I guess when Stacey got pregnant, when we got pregnant, well, we knew we loved each other and so the decision was kind of made for us."

"Do you ever wonder if you picked the right person? I mean, how do you know?" Chase asked, looking over at Nathan.

If it weren't for the earnest expression in the young man's eyes, Nathan might have been tempted to tell him to mind his own business, but the sincerity there convinced him otherwise. "No. I mean, yes, sometimes. Choices have to be made at the time, and you make them and then your life becomes your life. One day I wake up and I have a wife, a job, a house, and a couple of kids and it's like, when did that happen?"

Chase held his stare and nodded, seeming to comprehend the immensity of his experience. But how could he? He was a college kid.

"I sometimes wonder, if I was a teenager now instead of back then, if I would have made different choices," Nathan confessed.

"Like what?"

"Just different. People are a lot more open-minded now." Nathan took in the absurdity of the situation. He was a man in his late thirties, sharing the very problems that had been weighing on his mind with his son's best friend, a young man practically half his age. Why was it so easy to talk to Chase? He felt an inexplicable bond and simultaneously an unsettling sense that he was talking to a 2.0 version of himself. "I've never talked about that with anyone before."

"Your secrets are safe with me if mine are safe with you," Chase promised, then looked down smiling.

"What?" Nathan asked.

"Nothing," Chase laughed. "You just look like Tyler when you're deep in thought like that."

"You mean, he looks like me," Nathan corrected. "I'm the original."

They laughed and watched as the first stars began to appear in the night sky. Nathan enjoyed the easy nature of their time together. It was as simple to carry on a conversation with Chase as it was to sit in silence and just be. It looked like he and Tyler shared a taste in the company they liked to keep.

"I'm gonna call it a night. I want to get down that ladder while I can still see it." Chase laughed as he stood and made his way over to the edge of the roof. "Thanks for the beer, and the chat."

"No problem, it was nice. I'm glad you ended up staying in tonight," Nathan said, following Chase to the ladder.

Chase looked up at Nathan as he began his descent. "Me too. Good night, Mr. Davidson."

Nathan climbed down and pulled the ladder away from the house. He watched Chase cross the yard and enter the guest cottage, flicking on its lights. *Mr. Davidson. What are you thinking, old man?* Nathan entered the house and was surprised at how foreign it all seemed. All the collected knickknacks from over the years seemed to stare at him like alien things. Stuff, stuff, everywhere just stuff, and this was his life. A life that had been fastidiously designed, and as he looked around he realized how little it all meant to him. He was becoming detached. He loved his family very much, but the idea of pulling around the weight of all these years of memories and mementos seemed a burden.

Nathan grabbed a golf magazine off the coffee table in the living room and lay down on the couch. He flipped mindlessly through the magazine, barely registering the lush green courses and players profiled inside. He wasn't even halfway through when he tossed the magazine on the floor and shut his eyes. Resting his hands on his chest, he tried to regain the peaceful quiet his mind had captured on the roof. He lay there, resembling a corpse except for the deliberate, slow rise and fall of his chest as he tried to encourage a meditative state. After a few minutes he was successful, to a degree. The chatter had stopped at least, and what was left was a slow parade of images, some captured from memory and some imagined.

Nathan's eyes almost opened as he felt an unexpected sensation. He felt his body. He was really feeling it; he was aware of himself all the way down to his feet. He wiggled his toes and felt the socks around them. He felt the denim hugging his thighs and the cotton collar of his polo shirt gently pressing against the back of his neck. It was so simple and yet sensational. He'd been living in his head and had been denying the existence of his body, and he'd been doing it for so long he couldn't even recall when it had started.

Warmth gathered in his chest and spread slowly through his body. He could almost detect the tiny hairs on his arms and legs responding as the energy passed through him. The warmth collected in his stomach and moved down into his pelvis. Nathan felt the denim getting very tight there, and he realized he was very, very horny. As the parade of images continued to scroll through his mind, he slid one hand down his body and stroked the front of his jeans. He slid the other hand up and under his shirt, dragging it over his chest, imagining the whole time that the hands belonged to someone else. He couldn't even remember the last time he had pleasured himself, and the thrill of doing it in the open of his house added to the rousing danger of it. Being a family man was a lot different from being a bachelor. You couldn't just pull it out whenever you got the urge. That was the curious part; he rarely even felt the urge, as if he had neatly folded up his sex drive and packed it in a box. He didn't have to face it or deconstruct the sexual images in his head. He was free to focus on every other aspect of his life without distraction. And it had become easier over time. As a young man in his teens and twenties, all he could seem to think about was sex. As the years went on, it had become easier and easier to just ignore.

He unbuttoned the top of his jeans and stuffed his hand in, grabbing himself firmly. This was not so easy to ignore, and the urgent excitement in his gut made him clench his jaw and squeeze his eyes shut. He wanted the intangible temptations in his mind desperately, and he also desperately wanted them to leave him alone. Nathan exhaled a long frustrated breath and opened his eyes, letting them adjust to the reality of the room. The wooden beams on the ceiling, the rich merlot window dressings, and the faint smell of the leather couch beneath him. He pulled his shirt down and removed the hand from his pants, but it did little to relieve the hard-on straining distinctly against them. He'd go to bed, he decided, and swung his legs down off the couch.

Nathan entered the bedroom and noticed Stacey was already sleeping, a book fallen against her chest and her reading lamp still on. He crossed to the closet and undressed, throwing his shirt and jeans over a chair. He was already beginning to feel more himself as he slipped into the washroom and dressed his toothbrush with paste. Temptation got the best of him, and he soon had one hand in his boxer shorts as the other one brushed. He closed his eyes again, imagining another's firm grip around his balls. His breathing became rapid and shallow as he brushed harder and stroked faster.

"Nathan?" He heard Stacey call in a half-asleep voice from the next room. He pulled the hand out of his shorts and rested it on the sink, panting. He bent over and spit into the sink and rinsed his mouth. He looked in the mirror and smiled sardonically at himself.

"Yes?" he answered as he flicked off the washroom light and crossed to the bed.

"Are you coming to bed?" Stacey asked, closing her book and setting it on the nightstand.

Nathan answered by climbing in and turning off the lamp on his nightstand. Stacey turned and did the same. Nathan rolled over and curled into Stacey, rubbing his fingers along her arm. He pressed against her, and Stacey turned with surprise.

"Nathan?"

"You want to mess around?" he asked, already letting his hands rove over his wife.

"Now?"

"Or… we don't have to," Nathan answered, stopping his hands in place.

"No, I'd like to. But are you sure?" Stacey asked.

"Look, do you want to or not, Stacey?"

"You're not all that attractive when you're grumpy," Stacey accused, crossing her arms and leaning back against the headboard.

"Forget it." Nathan turned onto his side away from Stacey and stared at the wall.

"Come on, you just surprised me, that's all."

"I said forget it. I'm not in the mood anymore. I'm going to sleep."

CHASE STARED at the digital alarm clock on the nightstand beside his bed in the guest cottage. It read 9:59 p.m. Blinking, it turned to 10:00 p.m. He'd been lying on his bed watching the minutes click by since coming down off the roof with Nathan. He just couldn't make his mind up. He'd wanted to call Jarod all day but had repeatedly chickened out since swiping his number from Tyler's phone when Tyler was in the shower this morning. How would he even begin the conversation?

"Hey Jarod, it's Chase… yeah, the guy you made out with in the bushes last night…. I was just wondering if you wanted to… what?"

What if he denied it even happened? It wasn't like Jarod had handed Chase his number. Christie had been all over that. And then there had been the issue of how to explain to Tyler that he wanted to hang out with Jarod, and at this point, preferably alone. Tyler had headed to the movies with Bre, but then not quite so conveniently his dad had taken Chase at his word that he was too tired to go out and invited him for male bonding time. Which had turned out to be surprisingly… enjoyable. Mr. Davidson was so much like Tyler: funny, charismatic, and definitely handsome. It had been so comfortable talking with him, he almost felt like Mr. Davidson might understand if he brought up Jarod even more than Tyler might.

For a second Chase let his mind wander to his own father, whom he had barely known. He had to conjure up images of the man, memories he'd tried desperately to hold on to over the years and that were dangerously close to slipping away for good. He wouldn't have even remembered his father's voice if it weren't for the few family videos he had played repeatedly, especially in the early years following his death. Grainy camcorder footage of the two of them at the fire hall where his father had worked, decked out in matching firefighter gear. A four-year-old boy helping his daddy wash the fire truck. It was so surreal, as if that hadn't been him or his life at all but had belonged to someone else. It had been taken from him, and so all he had left were a few fleeting images of the man to cling to.

Chase pushed the memories of his father out of his head. He spent so much of his life reconstructing and analyzing the past, and he felt exhausted by it. He wanted to live the way he had last night—spontaneously. He wanted to feel again what it was like when all the thoughts stopped and he was left with only the sanctity of the moment. He wanted to see Jarod.

He picked up his phone for the umpteenth time that day and finally pressed the Call button where it had sat blinking on Jarod's name all day. And then he waited as it rang, his heart beating a staccato rhythm.

"Yup, it's Jarod."

"It's Chase. How's it going?"

"How'd you get this number?" The voice was a little gruff on the other end of the line.

"I uh, I swiped it from Tyler's phone," Chase admitted, already regretting all of this.

"Good work, super sleuth. I was just about to drive over there and get yours myself." Jarod was laughing now, and Chase couldn't help but join in, a sense of relief washing over him.

"Well, maybe you should drive over here anyway. I've not really seen much of the area, you know. You could be my tour guide." Chase was surprised at his coy response. Had he actually been smooth just now? *Don't get ahead of yourself, Romeo. You've only been at this a day.*

"Ten minutes. I've got a blue truck."

"Okay." Chase hung up and a terrifying excitement crept over him. Ten minutes? He walked to the floor-length mirror and decided that nothing reflected in it was working. He quickly stripped down and ran to the shower. Last night he was sure he had smelled like campfire, and he wanted to be sure he gave the best impression possible tonight. Chase smiled as the water splashed against his body. He imagined Jarod's lustrous brown eyes staring back at him and began to feel a warm sensation gathering in his stomach and spreading out through his body. Chase wasn't thinking anymore. He was simply swimming in this new emotion, and it felt great.

Chase stepped out of the shower and, grabbing a towel, stole a glance at the digital alarm clock. Five minutes and counting. He whipped the towel around his body, drying off faster than he'd imagined possible, and darted for the closet, which wasn't a closet at all but a thick wooden dowel hung on brackets. He and Tyler had hung all their clothes together. About halfway through the college year, they had given up on separate closets as so much borrowing and swapping had gone back and forth. It was easier to just take what was needed, wash, and return it to the communal hangers. This system had rarely caused a problem, usually when Chase had borrowed (or was wearing) a shirt that Tyler had in mind for a date. But in essence they had both doubled their wardrobe, so most grievances were set aside after some momentary grumbling. Chase had always felt that he had made out well in the agreement. Tyler's clothes always bore an enviable label while his own, well… didn't. Tyler didn't seem to notice, and Chase had never caught him pulling back a collar to examine a tag.

Chase flipped through the clothes and selected a baby blue polo of Tyler's. It had always been a favorite, and he thought it made Tyler's eyes appear even more blue, if that were possible. He pulled it on, grabbed a pair of jeans, and hiked them up, turning back to the mirror. No time for hair, he decided with another quick glance at the clock. He pulled on a navy ball cap and drew a deep breath, giving himself a nervous once-over in the mirror. *That's as good as it's gonna get in ten minutes.* He smiled at his reflection. Tonight, he was going on his first date with a guy.

Chase flicked off the light in the guest cottage and walked into the yard. The night air felt good; it was cooler than the evening had been on the roof but still warm enough for his short sleeves. He could smell the moonflowers and evening primrose hard at work blooming and spreading their fragrance on their night shift in the garden. The maple and poplar trees sang softly in the breeze, their leaves slipping against one another. Chase looked up and saw the stars that were only beginning to appear earlier in the evening sky now shining brightly. The moon was a glowing crescent and hung low over the lake, casting its beam across the water like a silvery boardwalk. He breathed in the night garden and whispered to himself a verse he had thought he'd long forgotten.

> *"Four days will quickly steep themselves in night;*
> *Four nights will quickly dream away the time;*
> *And then the moon, like to a silver bow*
> *New-bent in heaven, shall behold the night."*
> *A Midsummer Night's Dream.* It certainly felt like it.

JAROD'S BLUE truck idled in the driveway as Chase walked around the corner of the house. Jarod's attention was focused on the stereo, but he looked up and smiled when Chase tapped on the passenger window. He leaned over and opened the door. "Welcome to the finest sightseeing tour available around Prospect Lake."

Chase climbed up into the truck and was surprised to hear what was on the stereo. Rich violins and cellos were dueling between the left and right speakers. He knitted his eyebrows quizzically at Jarod.

"Yo-Yo Ma on Bach's Cello Suites. You don't like it?"

"No, it's beautiful, just not what I was expecting," Chase admitted.

"Just because I wear a jersey doesn't mean classical music doesn't bend my ear," Jarod said defensively. "Obviously we have a lot to learn about each other. Where do you want to start?"

"How about you show me your favorite spots around the lake," Chase suggested, buckling up.

Yo-Yo Ma's cello soared as Jarod pulled onto the street and headed down the twisty tree-lined road. Chase unrolled his window and let his hand play in the wind, trying to match it to the fluctuations in the music, dipping down as the music retreated and then climbing in a crescendo. He was lost in the perfect mathematics of the music when he felt a warm hand on his.

Chase turned and Jarod smiled, his eyes meeting Chase's for a moment before returning to the road. Chase looked down and interlocked their fingers, liking the way the different skin tones made a pattern. Feeling Jarod's rough skin excited Chase, and he rubbed his thumb over the back of his date's hand, enjoying the intimate detail of the little dark hairs there. Allowing his eyes to wander up Jarod's arm, he noticed the thickness of his forearms and how the muscles naturally stretched the cotton sleeves of his T-shirt. He wanted to run his hands up to Jarod's bicep and feel the firmness there. He blew out a breath and brought his eyes back to the road. His head was already swimming with all the pheromones in the truck.

"So where you taking me?" Chase asked.

"I was kind of thinking it would be safest for us to park as soon as possible. I'm having trouble keeping my mind on the road." Jarod laughed. "There's a great scenic spot at the top of Little Saanich Mountain to look down on the lake."

"Sounds good to me," Chase responded, and suddenly his heart was beating somewhere up near his throat. A lookout spot? That sounded conspicuously like the type of place where people went to make out. A bunch of cars with steamy windows parked in a row on a cliff. Hands tensed like cats' claws raking down through the condensation on the glass and a psychopath lurking in the woods with a murder weapon ready to cut them all to bits. Maybe he had seen too many horror films.

The truck wound up the gravel road on Grouse Mountain, and Chase rolled his window up. The air was getting cooler up here. Through the windshield the star-filled sky was only visible through intermittent breaks in the dense forest. Jarod slowed and turned off the main road onto an even narrower gravel path through the woods. They drove for another few minutes, and all at once the giant fir trees gave way to a clearing on the mountainside. The moon appeared to hang directly in front of them over the lake far below. There was no long line of fogged-up cars, only the two of them and Yo-Yo Ma's precise fingers recounting Bach's masterpiece.

"It's beautiful," Chase whispered, edging farther up in his seat to take in the view.

"I thought you'd like it," Jarod said, but his eyes weren't on the sky or the lake below; he was turned in his seat and looking at Chase. "So you stole my number, huh? Couldn't even wait for me to give it to you?"

Chase smirked. "Well, if you were a little more on the ball, I wouldn't have had to go digging. Christie beat you to it. You're just lucky I'm not out with her tonight."

"I'd say we're both lucky," Jarod said and reached for Chase's hand again, pulling him closer on the bench seat. Jarod slid over and they sat side by side in the old truck, ignoring the view and just taking in each other.

Chase slid his hand up the arm he'd been tempted by and held tight to the muscle there, smiling. "Work out much?"

"A little…." Jarod laughed and leaned in to kiss Chase's neck.

The warmth of Jarod's mouth on his throat made Chase's pulse race, and he closed his eyes in pleasure when the other boy's tongue flicked and explored around his ears. Chase dragged his hand down Jarod's arm and grabbed his thigh, massaging the muscle through his jeans. It was obvious Jarod spent a good amount of time training and in the gym; he was well-built all over.

Jarod kissed along Chase's jawline and paused on his chin, drawing his mouth up until he reached Chase's lips. They kissed softly, brushing their lips against each other while locking eyes. Chase stuck his tongue out slowly and licked Jarod's lips, curiously tasting him. Jarod patiently let him explore and then slipped his own tongue out so the two danced together.

Jarod rested his forehead against Chase's and whispered across the darkness, "Come on, let me show you the best dreaming spot around." He reached behind the seat and pulled out a black-and-blue plaid blanket, then hopped out of the truck.

Chase followed and watched Jarod climb up into the bed of the truck, carefully lay out the blanket, and then turn and offer him a hand up. "What exactly is a dreaming spot?" Chase asked as he grabbed Jarod's hand and felt himself pulled almost effortlessly up onto the tailgate.

"Let me show you, handsome," Jarod said and lay down on the blanket, folding his hands behind his head. Chase followed his lead and joined Jarod, one arm crooked comfortably behind his head and the other resting on Jarod's stomach. The fir trees seemed to stretch on forever into the night, and high above, long strokes of colored light chased each other across the sky. The tops of the trees were like pointed paintbrushes splashing iridescent hues over one another before fading into the blackness and beginning again.

"It's beautiful," Chase whispered. "I don't remember the last time I saw the northern lights."

"It happens pretty regularly out here, far away from the city," Jarod said, reaching one hand down and joining it with Chase's.

"I'm glad you came out to the fire last night. I was considering drowning myself in the lake before you showed up." Chase turned to look at Jarod. "How do you stand it?"

"What's that?"

"The constant lying, the pretending to be people that we're not."

"I'm not lying to anyone. I am who I am," Jarod said casually, but there was a defensive tone beneath the surface.

"Does anyone here know you like guys?" Chase challenged.

"Does anyone here know *you* like guys?" Jarod echoed.

"No."

"So why would they have to know? That's my business, not theirs."

"But these people are supposed to be our friends. Doesn't it feel like the friendship only goes so far when we're not telling the entire truth?" Chase asked, knowing the question was as much for himself as it was for Jarod. "I guess sometimes I just get tired of all the games."

Jarod rolled over and started tickling Chase. "What about this game? Are you tired of playing this game?"

"Yeowww! Stop it!" Chase howled as Jarod's fingers ravished him. "Okay, okay!"

Jarod rolled on top of Chase and held his hands above his head, then leaned down and kissed him. "Don't get all serious on me. Let's just have fun, okay?"

"Okay." Chase smiled back and, with the delicious weight of Jarod on top of him and the northern lights burning across the sky above them, agreed there was nothing to get upset about. How could anyone have a problem with something as beautiful as this?

IT WAS almost one in the morning when Jarod dropped Chase off. They had fallen asleep in each other's arms in the back of the truck, looking up at the dazzling summer sky. Jarod was right; it was a great dreaming spot. Chase crossed the yard and slipped into the guest cottage quietly, but he had beaten Tyler home. He couldn't help but smile as he undressed and thought about his night with Jarod. He was anxious to see him again already.

It was going to be a challenge to keep this a secret from Tyler. And wouldn't it just be easier if they told Tyler the truth? Sure, it might take some getting used to, but the whole idea of being out was going to take some getting used to for Chase too. Maybe he was being too quick with this whole idea of coming out. After all, it might be easier for *him* to come out in a place where he knew very few people. What about for Jarod? He'd spent his summers here since childhood, like Tyler. He probably knew half the people around the lake. Chase was considering coming out to Tyler, his family, and a small assortment of people he'd just met. And he'd just met Jarod for that matter. His spirits sank as he realized how irrational he was being. What right did he have to talk to Jarod about coming out? He barely knew the guy. "Don't get all serious on me. Let's just have fun…." Wasn't that what Jarod had said? Maybe it wasn't the same at all for Jarod. Maybe he didn't consider Chase relationship material but had just stumbled upon something convenient.

Chase climbed into bed and shook his head. That wasn't it. There was something special developing between him and Jarod. He had to believe in providence. It was too much of a coincidence otherwise. Obviously, they had been meant to meet last night, and obviously they were meant to spend their summer nights together….

Just then, Tyler walked in and interrupted Chase's daydreaming. He dove onto his bed and threw a pillow at Chase. "You're still up?"

"Couldn't sleep."

"That's because you're not getting any action. Unlike me, fully serviced, thank you," Tyler said, beaming a smile at Chase as if this information would impress him.

"Congratulations."

"Dude, what is wrong with you? You stay home and play board games instead of hooking up. Christie was probably waiting, primed for you like a cat in heat," Tyler said, taking a pillow and ramming his hips against it to emphasize his point.

"I'm just not into it," Chase answered, shaking his head at Tyler's freshman behavior.

"You know what they say, use it or lose it."

As Tyler got ready for bed, Chase considered his advice. Maybe Tyler was right. There was no reason he had to remain a virgin at the end of the summer. It just wouldn't be Christie who would be his undoing.

THE NEXT morning Chase awoke early and was inspired. It seemed his libido wasn't the only thing that had gotten a charge on the mountaintop the previous night. He slipped out of bed and crossed to the makeshift closet and dug through his duffel bag, pulling out his brushes, oils, and a folding easel. He had brought a selection of stretched canvases and fingered through the sizes that rested against the wall by his bed. He wasn't even sure what he would paint, but as he set up his workstation on the small patio outside the guest cottage, a muse caught his eye.

Mrs. Davidson was sitting in the breezeway of the house having her morning coffee and looking out over the lake. She appeared deep in thought as Chase got to work, careful not to alert her to his presence. He wanted to observe her just like this, in a private moment. And in that moment, which Stacey believed to be all her own, Chase noticed something. He noticed that his best friend's mother did not appear happy. In fact she appeared riddled with an age-old worry, one that was not easily put to rest.

STACEY STOOD at the counter slicing pears, peaches, and strawberries with rapid precision. After finishing the last of the fruit, she scooped it into separate serving bowls and placed them on the breakfast table. The Belgian waffles were grilled and staying warm in the oven, and the only item left to prepare was the whipped cream. She pulled out a large mixing bowl, poured in the cream, and flipped on her electric mixer.

Thankfully the buzz from the mixer helped to drown out the mental argument she'd been having with Nathan all morning. She knew it was ridiculous, this imaginary dialogue with her husband where she was able to disclose what she was really feeling and he was forced to listen. She also imagined all his excuses and accusations, which only further raised her blood pressure. But as always her kitchen provided a sanctuary, a place where she could begin the ritual of preparing food for her family, and soon the stress would float away as she immersed herself in new recipes.

Unfortunately this morning's menu didn't require a lot of concentration, as she knew it by heart and could have just as easily prepared it in her sleep. And so Stacey was finding it more difficult than usual to construct her Fucking Happy Face and keep it from slipping out of place. The FHF was the most valuable tool in her Superhero Mom tool kit, and when constructed properly it was impenetrable and the best diversion for not only her own family but the world at large.

Stacey flicked off the electric mixer. The cream had stiffened into little white peaks. She pulled a spatula from her utensil rack and flipped the fluffy white topping out into a proper serving bowl. She grabbed the counter in front of her as if for stability and strategically widened her eyes and lifted the corners of her perfect pink mouth up toward her ears before calling her family. "Breakfast!"

Birdy arrived with Tyler and Chase, and they assembled at the table. Stacey glided around and served orange juice. "Birdy, where's your dad?"

Birdy shrugged as she reached for a waffle and began dressing it with fruit. "Maybe he's running."

"Is he still doing that?" Tyler asked.

"Every day," Nathan answered, walking through the door, his T-shirt drenched in sweat. "Do something for twenty-one days and it becomes a habit."

"Well, wake me and Chase up tomorrow and we'll go with you."

Nathan headed toward the bedroom. "You guys couldn't keep up with me!"

"Yeah, right! Watch yourself, old-timer. You could accidentally trip out there," Tyler threatened.

"You know, a little endurance might help your golf game," Chase suggested wryly.

"You know, a little duct tape might make you shut up," Tyler answered, slapping Chase on the back of the head playfully. "And you're not allowed to coach me until you sink a few balls yourself, Chastity."

Stacey interrupted by stepping between the boys and offering fresh coffee. "Are you looking forward to working at the course, boys? Will it be challenging?"

"We're painting a fence, Mom. Not exactly putting our college education to use."

Stacey slammed down the pot of coffee between the boys. "I'm just trying to show interest and talk about something other than golf. There are other people at this table. Maybe you'd like to know what Birdy has planned for the day."

Tyler and Birdy exchanged bewildered glances at their mother's unusual terseness. Noticing Chase's shoulders had risen up toward his ears, Stacey quickly composed herself and fastened her FHF back in place. "Would anyone like some more waffles?" she asked with a smile.

Birdy looked at her mother incredulously. "We haven't even started yet."

"Well, we'd best get started, then, shouldn't we?" Stacey asked, taking her seat as Nathan arrived at the breakfast table in a clean, dry shirt.

"Your mother is right," Nathan commented, motioning for Tyler to pass him the coffee carafe. "It's polite to show interest. Otherwise we can seem cold or frigid."

Stacey flicked her linen napkin in the air and placed it on her lap. "Sometimes that's what people do when the actions of others seem erratic or unusual."

"It's difficult for a person to attempt spontaneity if they are greeted with ridicule," Nathan lectured, swirling sugar into his coffee and tapping the spoon on the edge of his cup.

"If you don't tend your chickens, they'll never produce a golden egg," Stacey said, stabbing a strawberry with her fork.

Tyler looked from his mother to his father, faced off at either head of the table. "Okay, okay. I get it. Show a little interest. Birdy, what do you have planned for the day?"

Birdy adopted the sarcastic tone of her parents as she poured syrup onto her mountainous morning creation. "Mom doesn't like that I saw a penis, so I'm going to start playing tennis."

"That sounds great, Birdy," Tyler said, stifling a laugh. "Great waffles, Mom, really great."

STACEY SAT in the courtside bleachers flipping through a magazine another parent had no doubt left behind. It was one of those celebrity-obsessed rags, and even though she dismissed it as drivel, she did shamefully find herself reading several articles with interest during Birdy's tennis lesson. Why was it that people were so preoccupied with the lives of others? She couldn't imagine what it would be like to have a life where all the world was truly a stage. And to have every makeup, breakup, possible pregnancy, and career up and down telegraphed on magazine stands across the nation. No, she preferred a quiet life without airing dirty laundry. She'd had her fair share of drama as a pregnant teenager. Surely that had provided enough trauma and back-fence talk for one lifetime.

Stacey set down the magazine and saw that Birdy was just finishing up with her tennis coach. They were holding the racquet together and practicing a swing. Birdy looked so adorable, dressed in a cute white skirt and matching polo, her hair pulled back in a ponytail. This was going to prove a much better option than those swimming lessons with the instructor who was obviously just there to collect a paycheck. He couldn't even be bothered to account for the kids in his class. Birdy's tennis coach was a confident and pretty teenage girl, someone for her daughter to look up to. Birdy came running over to Stacey, twirling the tennis racquet in her hands.

"Did you have fun?" Stacey asked, bending to retie her daughter's shoe.

"Yeah, Jenna is really cool."

"Good. I'm sure she'll be a positive influence for you," Stacey said confidently as she stood, noticing her daughter had her head still turned over her shoulder, watching Jenna as she changed her shoes courtside. Jenna looked up and waved.

"Yeah, she smells nice too," Birdy said, waving back enthusiastically.

"Well, we'd best hurry along. We need to get supplies for your burger night," Stacey said, taking Birdy by the hand.

"I don't want a burger," Birdy stated, her mind obviously made up. "Jenna is a vegetarian. She says eating animals is totally gross."

"Did she? That Jenna is quite the gal." Stacey quickened her step. She paid the girl for tennis lessons, not for sharing her philosophy on nutrition with her daughter.

CHASE DIPPED his paintbrush into the can and slapped the rich new forest green shade on the fairway fence. There was something very freeing about painting this way, one color, covering every past imperfection. No requirement for creativity or visualizing how it would all come together as a whole. It would be a green fence; that was it, no imagination needed. He'd begun to enjoy his time working on the golf course with Tyler. Their time mostly consisted of trimming trees, taking care of the greens, and raking out bunkers. It provided ample thinking time.

Tyler and Chase had been working on this fence all day in old jeans, sneakers, and ball caps, under the hot sun. Both had green streaks of paint across their arms, on their stomachs, and decorating their faces. This was a slop-it-on job, and in their haste as much paint found its way onto their bodies as onto the fence.

"You know, you should hit up Christie," Tyler said, dipping his brush into a can again and pulling it out sopping with paint up to the handle.

"Not really my type," Chase said, biting his tongue. Not this again. He had been hoping to get through the day without having to deflect Tyler's prodding efforts to get him to date.

"Man, don't be so soft. You don't have to marry her, just play like you mean it." Tyler laughed, grabbing a fence pole and pumping against it.

Chase dipped his brush in the paint and slapped it across the fence. "I don't wanna 'play.' I told you, I'm not into her. Just leave it alone."

"I'm calling Bre," Tyler said, pulling his cell phone out of the back pocket of his jeans. "She'll set you guys up for tonight."

"Tyler, just stop it, okay?"

"What? What's the matter with you, man?" Tyler asked, slowly letting the phone drop to his side.

"Listen, I should have told you this before. If you're gonna be mad and wanna kick me out or whatever I'd rather it be now." Adrenaline kicked in as the moment had come, and he had no intention of turning back.

"Chase, what are you talking about? Why would I kick you out?"

"Because if you can't deal with it, then I'd rather not be around you either."

"Dude, you're not making a whole lot of sense," Tyler said.

"We're friends, right?" Chase asked, catching Tyler's eye.

"You're my best."

"So it shouldn't matter, but I understand if it does, and I just don't want to pretend anymore. It's exhausting. So if you're gonna hate me, just fucking hate me and let's get it over with," Chase said, turning back to the fence.

"Are you gonna tell me what the hell you're talking about?"

"Tyler, I'm gay." He said it, and simultaneously wanted to suck the words back into his mouth and felt a huge weight lift from his shoulders. The hardest part was looking at Tyler to gauge his reaction.

"Yeah, right," Tyler said and laughed.

"Seriously, I am."

Tyler dipped his brush in the can and went back to painting. "No, you're not. You're shitting me, right?"

"Nope."

Tyler turned slowly and looked at Chase again. "Holy shit. For real? You're actually like... you like guys?"

"Yeah."

"Are you sure?"

"Yeah." Chase couldn't tell how Tyler was taking it. "Are you cool with this?"

"Yeah. Yeah. But I know you've been with girls... haven't you?" he asked.

"Been with... but not *been with*," Chase admitted.

"Have you been with guys?"

"Been with but not *been with*," Chase said again, even though it had really only been one guy, and recently. He hoped Tyler wasn't going to probe him for more specific details.

"Oh my God. This is soooo... I don't even know what this is. It's crazy. But if you've never really been with anyone, how do you know you're gay? You're a virgin. You're nothing yet!" Tyler rambled, beginning to pace.

"Tyler, I know."

"My best friend is gay," Tyler said to himself, staring at the grass under his feet.

"It doesn't mean you are."

"I know that."

A silence fell between them. After a few moments they went back to painting. Chase wasn't quite sure whether to pick up the conversation or begin another one. Most topics seemed pretty insignificant after this news.

"So are we cool?" Chase finally asked.

"Yeah, it's cool."

Unfortunately Tyler's answer didn't inspire a ton of confidence in Chase. Maybe Jarod had been right. Maybe it had been a mistake to tell him. At least he hadn't broken Jarod's trust and spilled his secret as well. As Chase looked at the long stretch of fence still to be painted, he became excited despite Tyler's mixed reaction. With his secret out in the open, his life seemed to stretch forward like a blank canvas, infinite in its possibilities.

CHASE STOOD behind his easel and watched as the young boy crouched with his net in the water, waiting for a minnow to swim into what could only be an unfortunate future with a seven-year-old boy. The long branches of the willow tree hung down and teased the surface of the lake with their leaves, creating a perfect shadowed cove for the boy to play in. Off to one side was a thick patch of cattails and lily pads, many of them in perfect pink and yellow bloom. No doubt there were all kinds of creatures lurking in there just ripe for the picking.

Chase pulled his trowel from his back pocket and squeezed out some dark beige to mix in with the ocher on his wooden palette to perfect the ruddy tan of the boy's shoulders. The young fisherman had been there for nearly an hour and didn't seem to mind or take notice of the painter taking inspiration from his playtime. Chase's brush worked fervidly across the canvas. He was in his groove, and his hands went about using the oils to capture the activity before him.

Chase couldn't recall a time when he was as carefree as this boy appeared. When his father had passed away, he'd felt sucked into the world of adults, ripe with the possibility of misfortune. He was sure some kids didn't realize their sexuality at such a young age, but he'd known there was something different by the time he was six. Maybe most kids didn't think about it because if you're straight, there's nothing to consider. But Chase had felt a bond with his swimming teacher when he was six. He couldn't explain it at the time, but he'd known he liked the tan of his skin and the sound of his laugh. What was becoming clear now was the parallel between the time of his father's death and his own awakening desires. The problem with even beginning to hypothesize on his own psychology was that he always found himself stuck between two contradictory views on sexuality. Was he hyper reacting to a traumatic event in his pre-oedipal stage, or was it the more convenient, more soothing belief that he was born this way? Could it be a combination of the two? He didn't see why not, although it didn't compartmentalize his past into little boxes he could easily label and stack away. He could incite some pretty passionate conversations about nature versus nurture if he walked a psychologist through his childhood. Not that he was looking to get into any more excitement than he'd already had today. Coming out to Tyler had been monumental, and he was still swimming in the surreal quality of an afternoon post closet.

He smiled as the boy scooped his net out of the water and it wriggled with a minnow. The boy ran to a pail he had placed at the water's edge and dumped the small swimmer into it. He cast his net to the ground, picked up the pail, and then dashed up the hill to the house next door. He was obviously anxious to share his trophy catch with someone at home.

Chase wiped his hands on his jeans and picked up the canvas and easel. His muse had gone home for the day and so too would he. Chase walked up to the house and around to the garage where he guessed he might find some supplies to clean up. He now had the combined efforts of fence and canvas painting across his hands and arms.

Considering the wet paint marring him, Chase pulled off his T-shirt and wrapped his hand in it, then tried the side door to the garage. He found it unlocked. Tossing the T-shirt over his shoulder, he crossed to the workbench and began to nose around, opening drawers and scanning the labels of the plastic bottles on the shelves.

"Looking for something?" The voice startled him, and Chase almost jumped out of his skin.

"Geez! You scared me!" he said, turning to see Nathan, sitting in his Porsche and watching him through the windshield.

"Sorry, I was taking a time-out I guess," Nathan said, climbing out of the car.

"I was just looking for some rags to clean up," Chase said sheepishly, ashamed now for nosing around in Nathan's workshop. "I should have asked first, but I didn't want to go in the house like this."

"It's no problem, whatever you need," Nathan said as he opened a drawer Chase hadn't searched yet and pulled out some rags. He set them on the workbench, then, noticing something, grabbed one. "Hold still, you've got some paint in your hair."

Chase stood still as Nathan pulled at a few strands of his hair with the rag. He hadn't noticed how much bigger than himself Nathan was, but standing this close it was clear he was a good deal taller. "You must be what... six two? Six three?"

"Six four, actually," Nathan said, lowering the rag and meeting Chase's eyes. "It doesn't do me a lot of good. I just hit my head on things a lot more. You're just cleaning up now? I thought you guys got home from working at the golf course a while ago."

"We did. I'm working on a new piece, just started this afternoon, actually," Chase explained, grabbing one of the rags and wiping his hands.

"Can I see it?"

"Umm yeah, okay. It's not done, though," Chase said, leading the way out of the garage. He stopped at the side of the house where he'd left the canvas on the easel and pointed shyly. "Well, that's it."

He couldn't read Nathan's expression. Nathan looked at the painting for a long time without saying anything, then turned to Chase and smiled. "You've got a gift. I mean it."

Chase looked up at Nathan and saw the man was sincere. "Thank you." He smiled and felt all the emotion that he'd kept bottled up that day rushing forward. All he'd ever wanted was to be accepted, to be recognized and appreciated. Nathan, with his time and a few simple words, had given him all of that.

"Go get cleaned up. Stacey's planned a barbecue. The neighborhood is bound to be showing up soon." Nathan laughed.

Chase watched Nathan walk across the patio and into the house. He wondered if Tyler realized how lucky he was.

TYLER SAT on the kitchen counter eating a carrot, watching his mom and Birdy prepare salads for the barbecue. When his mother had guests over it was never a simple affair, although she always made it seem like one. There would be an abundance of food.

Birdy stood at the kitchen island mixing one of the salads, but her mind was obviously elsewhere. "Can I get my ears pierced like Jenna's? She has three holes in each ear."

"Birdy, focus on mixing that salad, our guests will be here shortly," their mother instructed, sliding a pile of chopped celery off her cutting board and into Birdy's bowl. "We still need to make up the hamburger patties."

"Mom! I can't eat hamburger!" Birdy looked at her mother incredulously.

"Tyler, will you please go to the store and get some veggie burgers for Birdy? She's decided not to eat meat anymore. And if you see your dad, ask him to light the barbecue," his mom asked, expertly carving into a pineapple.

Tyler jumped off the counter and headed to the garage, yelling, "Dad! You need to light the barbecue!"

TYLER WALKED into the garage and saw his father sitting in his car, hands on the wheel. "Dreaming of the autobahn?"

"Oh, hey. Yeah, just hanging out." His dad turned and smiled.

"I need to get some veggie burgers for Birdy. You wanna come with?" Tyler asked.

"Sure. Whose car?"

"If you let me drive, let's take yours," Tyler suggested, and his father tossed him the keys.

It was a short drive to the Red Barn, the local grocery store. Tyler was preoccupied, but his father seemed to be too, so the radio was a comfort, preventing any awkward silence. Tyler was still reeling from Chase's revelation this afternoon. He wasn't sure how he was supposed to feel; he knew he was confused and a little hurt. He felt lied to. Why didn't Chase just tell him in the first place? If he liked guys, fine, no big deal, but now Tyler was feeling like an idiot. Bits of memories were floating in and out of his mind from their past year together, plenty of opportunities for Chase to have come out to him. It cheapened what he had thought they had somehow.

Tyler had envisioned them as true best buddies who had fun and shared everything. In light of today's information, the friendship was feeling a little one-sided. He'd always been open with Chase, answered any and every question honestly.

As Tyler pulled into the parking lot of the Red Barn, he decided that was the issue. He was hurt that Chase hadn't trusted him enough to tell him the truth a long time ago. Tyler parked the car, and he and his dad walked into the grocery store. Tyler grabbed a basket by the door.

"Soy or mixed vegetable matter?" his father asked, pointing at the options in the cooler with a grimace on his face.

"Let's take the soy, it looks a little safer. Vegetable matter? What's that?" Tyler took two of the soy and placed them in his basket. "So, no more meat for Birdy…. She's so weird sometimes."

His dad continued walking down the vegetable aisle, selecting some tomatoes and placing them in a bag. "Maybe she just needs a change."

"But she's always eaten meat. Why decide today?"

"Maybe she never really liked it," his dad suggested, placing the bag of tomatoes in their basket.

"Do you think after she gets a taste of it, she'll go back?" Tyler asked, following his father as he selected heads of lettuce.

"Don't know. Maybe she'll be a veggie for life. Maybe you should try it. You might surprise yourself."

"Nope, don't need to try it," Tyler decided, picking up the soy burgers again for inspection. "Look at that. How could anybody eat that?"

"Quit playing with your sister's food. Are we done here?"

"Dad, can I ask you something?"

"Shoot."

"Chase… he, um… he came out to me today. And I'm okay with it. I mean, I was surprised, but the whole time I was just thinking to myself, 'Say the right thing, say the right thing.' And I have no idea if I did. It doesn't change anything between us, but it kind of changes everything. You know what I mean?" Tyler looked up at his father, hoping for some kind of advice, any kind of advice. "What do you think I should do? I mean, what am I supposed to do now?"

His dad looked at him for a second as if considering his options before answering, "Same thing you did yesterday."

"What do you mean?"

"Chase is your best friend, right? Just keep being that for him."

WHEN TYLER and his father arrived home from the Red Barn, Tyler noticed their neighbors had already begun to gather in the backyard, a stunning craggy hillside broken up by manicured gardens tended to by Stacey's meticulous horticultural thumb. Birdy was blowing bubbles as a couple of boys around her age chased each other around the yard with water guns. Stacey was busy serving drinks to the guests around the table on the patio. Marty, the owner of the golf course, and his grandson, Felix, had taken up residence close to the barbecue, no doubt anxious to talk shop with Nathan. Neighbors Jim and Jacky sat side by side at the table, already sipping on a beer and a long island iced tea respectively. Nathan and Stacey had been friends with Jim and Jacky for nearly as long as they had owned the lake house. Tyler had practically grown up with their son, Jarod, in the summers.

Tyler greeted the family friends and pulled up a chair beside Bre, who held a stem of white wine and seemed to be enjoying the comfortable banter between cottagers. He gave her a quick kiss on the cheek as he settled in.

"So, you play a round today, Nathan?" Jim asked as Nathan flipped open the barbecue lid and bent down to light it.

"We're not going to talk about golf tonight, Jim. We're going to talk about other interests," Nathan informed his friend with a wry smile.

"Bad game?" Marty and Felix suggested simultaneously.

"No. New family policy. Stacey introduced it this morning," Nathan explained with a little look over his shoulder at Stacey, who was setting a tray of cut vegetables on the table.

"I was only pointing out that sometimes it's nice to include other people in the conversation. People like Birdy and me, who don't play golf."

"Maybe you two should take it up," Marty chimed in, always on the lookout for new club members.

"I know exactly what you mean," Jacky complained, tapping her glass to signal Stacey she was ready for her next martini. "In our house it's football. Football twenty-four seven. I may as well live in a dugout."

"Sidelines. You may as well live on the sidelines. There are no dugouts in football." Jim laughed.

"Either way, I agree with Stacey. There are other things to talk about besides sports. When's the last time you asked me about my interests?" Jacky asked her husband, raising an eyebrow accusingly.

"I'll start asking about your interests when you take an interest in football," Jim offered.

Stacey interrupted the impending argument by shaking the martini mixer loudly and taking Jacky's glass. "Well, today Birdy started tennis lessons."

"That's great!" Jacky exclaimed, although the excitement may well have been more about her refilled glass.

"Maybe," Stacey stated flatly, sitting for the first time with her own martini.

"Maybe?" Tyler asked, Bre hanging on his arm as he grabbed a carrot stick from the veggie tray.

"She seems to have a fascination with her coach. I don't know if it's healthy."

"I'm sure he's harmless. It's probably just a little crush." Jacky said, pushing away any concern with a flip of her hand in the air.

"*She* looks harmless, but that's all Birdy can talk about since the lesson. Jenna this and Jenna that," Stacey explained, looking pointedly at Jacky across the table.

Tyler just laughed. The last thing he could imagine was his little sister being gay, though after the revelation with Chase, anything seemed possible. "Oh, come on, Mom. I have a man crush on Brad Pitt, doesn't mean I'm gay." As he said it, Tyler noticed Chase and Jarod standing a few feet away, within earshot of this entire conversation.

"I just want Birdy to have a normal childhood," his mother said, grabbing a celery stick and fixatedly chewing on it.

Bre looked around the table and shrugged. "I don't think it's bad to be gay. I think it's totally normal."

Tyler's mom looked at his girlfriend, surprised at being reprimanded. "I'm not saying it's bad, I just don't know that I want Birdy to be… like that. It would be easier for her if she wasn't."

"I sure as hell wouldn't want a son of mine to be growing up queer," Jim stated, taking a swig of his beer.

"Jim!" Jacky elbowed him in the ribs.

"Well, I wouldn't."

Tyler watched as his mother looked around the table and then at his little sister, still blowing bubbles on the lawn. "Birdy can be anything she wants to be. I'd just prefer if she wasn't a lesbian."

"All right! Burgers are done, come and get 'em!" his father announced, turning from the barbecue with a plate full and shooting a pointed look at Stacey. "I'm so glad we're not talking about golf."

CHASE PULLED his burger apart, eating it in small pieces. After overhearing the conversation on the patio, he really wasn't that hungry. Quite the opposite actually; it had made him feel nauseous. What was he doing here? He didn't know these people, not really. At least he had Jarod now; that was a relief, having someone who understood what he was going through and what this roller coaster of emotions was really like. Jarod sat beside him on the sand, already working on his second burger. They had snuck away after grabbing their food, seeking some privacy down at the beach far below the cliff the house stood on, away from the neighbors' eyes and sharp tongues.

"I told Tyler today," Chase admitted, discarding the rest of his bun and stabbing the pieces of burger with a fork.

Jarod almost choked. "You what?"

"I told Tyler. Just about me. I couldn't stand it anymore. He was going on and on about Christie, and I just did it."

"What did he do?" Jarod asked, setting down his food. His full attention was on Chase now.

"I think he took it okay. He couldn't believe it at first, but he didn't flip out or anything. I mean, I'm still here, right?" Chase tried a laugh, but it came out a little strained.

"You didn't say anything about us, right?" Jarod asked, a muscle in his jaw slightly twitching.

"No. Of course not, we made a promise. I wouldn't break that," Chase assured him, feeling even more alone than before.

"Good. It's all good. You do what you gotta do. But for me it's on the DL. I still have my eye set on getting drafted, and I've never heard of anyone being out in the top four sports," Jarod said, his gaze drifting off to the horizon. This was obviously something he'd thought about a lot.

"The top four?" Chase asked.

"Football, basketball, hockey, and baseball," Jarod explained, giving Chase a wink. "Sorry, champ, golf doesn't count."

"Damn it. You just trashed all my dreams of going pro!" Chase laughed. "I *work* at the golf course, I don't play. You obviously haven't seen me in action."

"Not in golf." Jarod smiled and, with a quick look around to be sure the beach was clear, leaned over for a kiss. "You wanna toss the ball around?"

"You know, I imagined this would be part of the criteria to hang out with you," Chase said, setting down his plate and following Jarod farther onto the sand.

"Let's see what you got," Jarod challenged, tossing a perfect spiral to Chase. "You might be a Terry Bradshaw."

Chase caught the ball and threw it back; it wobbled but thankfully reached its mark. He watched as Jarod danced around some imaginary opponents and fired off another bullet toward him.

"Or maybe you're a Lynn Swann or a Franco Harris," Jarod suggested, watching with hands on hips as Chase fumbled the ball.

"I don't really know who any of those guys are," Chase admitted.

"I have so much to teach you!" Jarod laughed and then ran at Chase, who did his best to get away.

Jarod proved too fast and tackled Chase to the ground, leaning over him on all fours. Chase looked up at Jarod's smiling mug and grinned. "I like this game."

Jarod leaned in for a quick kiss and then stood, giving Chase a hand up and passing off the football. Just as Chase turned to walk away, Jarod bear-hugged him from behind and kissed his neck. Chase slowly turned and leaned into Jarod, enjoying the sensation of being wrapped up in his strong arms. "Are we done playing?"

"We're done playing with the football." Jarod grinned.

"What happened to you being on the DL? Feeling awful brave all of a sudden… or are you realizing you're powerless against me?" Chase asked, cocking one eyebrow coyly.

"I know what I'd like to be doing to you right now," Jarod said, leaning in and biting Chase's ear gently.

"Oh yeah, what's that?"

"Well, we can't do it here…."

"Must be something pretty private, then," Chase guessed.

"It is," Jarod whispered, resting his forehead against Chase's. "My folks are heading back to the city for a couple weeks…. Maybe you should come over."

"Maybe I will," Chase agreed, leaning in to kiss Jarod again.

"Anyone want a—"

Jarod pulled away from Chase and wheeled around to see Christie holding two beers and looking back and forth between them with a confused look on her face.

"I told you to stay away from me!" Jarod spit at Chase, distancing himself even further. He bent to pick up the football and walked over to Christie, taking one of the beers. Christie shot a look over her shoulder at Chase as Jarod wrapped an arm around her shoulders and quickly started walking her back up the beach.

"What happened?" Chase heard her ask, her eyes still on him.

"Nothing. He just tried something, and I set him straight," Jarod said, quickening his step.

CHASE LET the sand run through his fingers again. He'd been doing this for nearly an hour, not sure what his next move should be. He was scared to leave the beach and also very scared to be alone. Because that was how he felt now more than any other time in his life: absolutely, completely, and utterly alone. He knew he should do something—at least move from his crouched position in the sand. His legs had long ago fallen asleep, and the numbness had spread through his body, creating an aching well when it reached his heart. It was as if a black hole had been created in the center of his chest, and everything that had been so beautiful and exciting about the world an hour ago was now being sucked into the bottomless dark pit inside him. Chase prayed that he too would be sucked into the dark chasm within and disappear. It would be a hell of a lot easier than walking up the steps and facing the people at the barbecue, who he was sure would now all be staring at him with narrowed eyes, if they hadn't already gathered their pitchforks to drive him from town.

He knew he had to stand and make his way up the hill. Dusk had fallen and soon it would be dark. Surely most of the neighbors had already gone home. Chase smoothed out the pile of sifted sand and slowly pushed himself to his feet. Pinpricks danced up and down his legs. He rocked back and forth and kicked his feet to start the blood flowing again.

"You okay?"

Chase turned to see Tyler walking up the beach toward him.

"Yeah, I'm fine. My legs just fell asleep...."

"I thought maybe *you* fell asleep. You've been gone a long time," Tyler said as he reached Chase and looked him up and down. "Fine, huh? You know what my mom says fine stands for? Fucked up, insecure, neurotic, and emotional. So, are you fine?"

Chase couldn't help but laugh but was surprised as tears filled his eyes at the same time. "Pretty much. Your mom said that?"

"Well, she had been drinking at the time. Forget about it, dude. Jim doesn't know his head from his ass and my mom… she just wasn't thinking." Tyler reached his arm around Chase's shoulder and gave him a squeeze. "It'd be totally different if she knew."

"Oh right. That." Chase felt another little twist in his gut, although it was nothing compared to his bruised feelings over Jarod.

Tyler bent down and picked up a handful of stones, handing some to Chase. He leaned back and then fired one from his hip, skipping it across the water. Chase tossed one of the stones up and down in his hand and then followed Tyler's lead casting it into the lake. "So, is everybody still up there or did they go home?" Chase asked.

"Most have gone home."

"Jarod and Christie?"

"Yup, left about an hour ago, said they were going to catch a movie."

"Is that all they said?"

"Yeah. What's up, Chase?"

Chase skipped another rock and then turned to look at his friend. "It's kind of like being a spy."

"What is?"

"Being gay. Because nobody knows for sure until I tell them. People will be brutally honest because they think nobody's listening, but I'm standing right there."

"Why didn't you tell me sooner? It's been bugging me."

"I didn't know how you'd take it. If you'd be okay seeing me with a dude," Chase said, looking out at the water. After a few moments he sat down in the sand, and Tyler joined him. The sun had dipped low on the horizon and sat like a colossal orange sinking into the lake. They sat in silence, watching the sky performing its evening light show. Eventually Tyler spoke, still looking out over the rippling water, now alive with the fire of the setting sun.

"I, ummm… I love you, man. I just want you to know that. But not like…."

"I know, no sword fights," Chase finished for him. "I love you too."

"Maybe we can think of a little more macho way to say it though…."

"Go Steelers?" Chase suggested after a few moments.

"Yeah, perfect. Go Steelers." Tyler tried it out. "Geez. That's the first time I ever said *that* to a guy."

"Me too," Chase said, realizing how much he loved Tyler, how thankful he was for the friendship, and how truly far he was from being alone.

NATHAN PEEKED into Birdy's room and noticed the light was still on in her loft. Of all the rooms in the lake house, this was one of his favorites. The ceiling was two stories up, and the walls were floor-to-ceiling bookshelves stocked with leather-bound volumes of his favorites, some dating back to his childhood. There was a converted loft up and over one of the walls of books, accessible only by a sixteen-foot ladder. Birdy had voiced claim to the space as hers long ago, and as soon as she was old enough to make the trek up and down the ladder safely by herself, Nathan and Stacey had granted her the space and the fairy-tale-like privacy it provided.

"Are you still awake, Pickle?" Nathan asked, crossing to the ladder.

"I want to find out what happens to Boo and Scout," she called over the library wall.

Nathan smiled to himself as he climbed the ladder. He remembered the intrigue of discovering those characters as a child too. Boo Radley, the mysterious and reclusive young man who lived next door.... At least she hadn't discovered his old copy of *The Well of Loneliness* by Radclyffe Hall. That would only lead to questions, and more questions from his daughter would likely put Stacey into a state of panic after this afternoon's hysterical talk about Birdy's budding sexuality—whatever it was.

Nathan poked his head over the library wall and looked into Birdy's loft, bathed in soft light from her reading lamp. She was tucked into bed and surrounded by a stuffed animal menagerie, her eyes not leaving the pages of the worn copy of *To Kill a Mockingbird*. "Hi, Dad," she said, flipping a page.

Nathan climbed into the loft and stooped to avoid hitting his head as he walked over to Birdy's bed. "What's happening?"

"He just saved Jem and brought him home," Birdy said, looking up at Nathan. "Can I get my ears pierced like Jenna's?"

"We'll have to talk with Mom. How did you like your veggie burger tonight?" Nathan asked, running a hand softly over Birdy's hair.

"I didn't. It tasted like sand," she admitted, scrunching her nose.

"Well, if you didn't try it, how else would you know, right? It's good to try new things."

"Yeah, I guess. How come Chase is staying with us? Why doesn't he spend the summer with his own family?" Birdy closed her book but kept a finger in place. "Brian says it's because his parents probably hate him."

"That's not true, Pickle. His dad died when he was a little boy, and he doesn't really get along with his mom, so this summer we're like his family," Nathan explained.

Birdy seemed to digest this information and file it somewhere for further processing. "Can I get my ears pierced tomorrow?"

Nathan just smiled at his daughter and shook his head. "We'll talk about it in the morning, sweetheart. Good night." He gave her a kiss on the forehead and headed down the ladder. "Don't stay up all night!"

"I won't, last chapter, I promise!" Birdy called out. "Night, Dad, love you."

"Love you too." Nathan turned out the light in the library and closed the door. He was quite content if the worst he had to consider was his daughter staying up late reading. She'd be a teenager soon enough, and he knew what would be on the boys' minds during high school. Then again, maybe he wouldn't have teenage boys to worry about….

THE SUN was still peeking over the horizon as Nathan's sneakers squished the dewy grass as he walked across the yard to the guest cottage. He intended to show the boys that he was more than capable of keeping pace with them after Tyler's snide remarks at the breakfast table yesterday. Nathan quietly snuck inside and stood between the two twin beds. The sheets were twisted and pulled into ropes on Chase's bed, and his pillow lay on the floor; he was evidently an active sleeper. His tan skin stood out in contrast against the white sheets, looking warm to the touch.

Nathan turned to Tyler's bed, where his son lay on his back with his arms splayed and jaw hanging slack, ready to catch flies. He grabbed Tyler's big toe and gave it a yank. Tyler gave a little kick and then rolled over, mumbling incoherently.

Chase woke up, startled when he saw Nathan. "Hey!"

Nathan jumped back as well and then tried a half whisper. "Morning. Sorry, didn't mean to startle you. Wake-up call. Time to run!"

Chase untwisted his limbs from the rolled sheets and climbed out of bed, stretching his arms up to the ceiling. Nathan couldn't help but let his eyes trace the lean muscle of Chase's chest and stomach down to the waistband of his red boxer shorts. Chase walked over to the sink, splashed water on his face, and then stuck a toothbrush in his mouth, talking around it. "Hey, sleeping beauty. Time to get up. Your dad is ready to run."

Nathan looked down to Tyler, who still didn't respond. He took a seat on the edge of Tyler's bed and sat waiting, his eyes furtively slipping up from the place on the floor where he tried to keep them trained to Chase leaning over the sink. The sunlight beginning to stream through the window made the blond hair on his tan legs glimmer. His little horseshoe-shaped triceps flexed as he leaned over the sink to rinse his mouth. It was a simple moment, just a morning routine, but for some reason it was captivating and... beautiful.

Chase walked past Nathan to the open closet and pulled out some shorts and a tank top. He slipped on the shorts and sat across from Nathan on his own bed to tie his sneakers. His forearms flexed as he tightened the laces, and he slung the tank top over his shoulder, only increasing the swimming sensation in Nathan's head. "Yo, Tyler! Let's go!" Chase said, rising and giving the lump of Tyler's body under the covers a shake.

"Go without me! Seriously, Dad, you're insane. No human should be awake right now." Tyler moaned and rolled over, pulling his pillow over his head.

Chase smiled at Nathan. "All right. Me and you, then."

THE SOFT crunch of gravel created a steady beat as Chase and Nathan jogged down the tree-lined path. Sunlight intermittently flickered through the giant trees, giving whole patches of earth an ethereal glow and leaving others swimming in shadows. They had been jogging for about fifteen minutes, in silence, one occasionally falling back and allowing the other to lead before leapfrogging again. Nathan felt self-conscious when he was leading the excursion. Second-guessing whether the pace was too fast or too slow, hoping it was neither and that Chase wasn't "jogging" just to be polite at a pace he could do a brisk walk to.

Though these worries troubled his mind while up front, they all dissipated as soon as he fell behind. Then most thoughts left his mind completely, and he was left staring and chasing after those little blue-and-gold running shorts as they cut through the woods.

His mind had been abuzz since Tyler told him about Chase. He was thinking irrationally, even inappropriately. He wanted to tell Chase a thousand things, a thousand thoughts he'd had, and ask a thousand questions too. It was all making sense now, why he'd felt the inexplicable connection. And after twenty years of marriage and a lifetime of trying to keep temptations away, here was the very epitome of temptation living under his roof. It had been one thing when Chase arrived, and Nathan felt a catch in his throat and a warm sensation creeping through his body. He was able to compartmentalize that into a little box and label it as "attractive, unattainable, and inappropriate—Do Not Touch." But now, the box had a new label: "attractive, potentially attainable, and inappropriate." He was having difficulty allowing that last part of the description to keep him from ripping off the "Do Not Touch" warning.

Nathan wasn't ready to make a statement like Chase had; he couldn't imagine it. It would destroy his family, his reputation, and his whole identity as he perceived it. He wasn't even sure that the label was the right one for him; he had never been with anyone but Stacey. So obviously he wasn't gay, but how to explain away these recurring and persistent fantasies? Especially when Chase was wearing those blue-and-gold shorts that hugged him all too well in all the right places and was jogging right in front of him.

There was a small clearing up ahead, and Chase slowed as they approached it. He turned around, beaming a satisfied smile at Nathan. "I needed this! Just thought we could stop for a few minutes and stretch."

"How's the pace? I'm not holding you back, am I?" Nathan asked, joining Chase in the clearing.

"No! Are you kidding? I was worried I was holding you back!" Chase laughed. "You're in amazing shape…."

"For an old guy."

"I wasn't going to say that."

"*I* said it. It's okay, I know. I'm almost twice your age." Nathan shook his head. "You know, sometimes I forget. I still feel young, you know? And then I catch myself in a mirror and think when the hell did that happen? The body changes, the mind doesn't."

"Can I use your shoulder?" Chase asked, pulling one leg behind himself.

"Uh, yeah, sure." Nathan's voice caught in his throat as Chase grasped his shoulder for balance. He looked down and saw the beads of sweat running down the young man's temples. Chase had pulled his tank top off early in the run, and it hung half tucked into the side of his shorts.

"Grab my shoulder and you can do the same," Chase instructed, glancing around the woods. "It's beautiful out here, huh?"

Nathan's gaze fell over the tan shoulders and chest below him. "Yeah."

Chase let one leg drop and switched, grabbing on to Nathan's other shoulder. He looked up at Nathan as he did. "Whoa, you're huge. I mean, I knew you were tall, but standing this close you're like a giant."

"Six foot four, remember?" Nathan answered, his voice coming huskily from deep in his throat. It was taking all the self-control he could muster not to pounce on Chase like some kind of wild animal. His mind was going fast in one direction, and the delicious scent of Chase's sweat was swirling infuriatingly in his nostrils and making him lasciviously mad.

"That's big." Chase laughed. "So, if I'm like five eight… that's like…."

"Eight inches," Nathan said, and almost died. "Difference I mean, between us, there's an eight-inch difference." He was sure the blood was running straight to his face. Was he actually blushing? Schoolgirls did that, not thirty-six-year-old men.

"So that's eight inches? It's bigger than I thought." Chase laughed, letting go of Nathan's shoulder. "The difference between us, I mean! Wow, okay, let's chalk that one up to awkwardly funny conversations to have with your best friend's father."

Nathan let the silence breathe between them as Chase squatted into a lunge, stretching his hamstrings. A swirl of thoughts jumbled his mind, so many things he wanted to say. "Chase, Tyler told me…."

Chase glanced up at Nathan momentarily and then went back to stretching. "I figured he would. I thought maybe you already knew."

"How would I already know?"

Chase looked up at him again and then grinned, shaking his head. "Well, I mean, you saw my sporting abilities, right? Must have been your first clue."

"Doesn't mean anything. I'm sure there are lots of… you know, I mean, I'm sure lots of guys who are good at sports… and also like other guys. Doesn't mean anything." Nathan stumbled over his words. He was sounding like an idiot. "Anyway, it's great you could talk to him. Times have really changed."

"Yeah, I guess," Chase said, standing and lunging onto his other leg.

"I bet you wish your dad was here for this," Nathan said, silently congratulating himself on getting a coherent sentence out. "You know you can always…. If you want to talk, I'm here, okay?"

Chase gave up on his stretching and stood for a few moments in silence, his eyes brushing over the ground in front of him. "I think about him a lot. What he was really like, what parts of him I have in me. My mom says I have his eyes, but that's all she's told me. She doesn't talk about him. After a while I got confused between my memories of him and stories I'd heard as a kid. I actually believed for the longest time he had given me magic beans to grow a beanstalk that would take me to him. How funny is that? You're so impressionable when you're a kid; your brain just soaks up

67

everything. And everything is real, because nobody tells you any different. And then one day you wake up and realize you really don't have any magic beans, that you never really had any and that your dad isn't ever going to come home. Funny, huh?"

Chase took a deep breath and turned away from Nathan, looking into the shadow-filled trees. After a few moments, he turned back with a smile, but it didn't hide the glistening in his eyes. "Okay, let's get running! We're gonna miss breakfast!"

Nathan took a deep breath, trying to find the right words for what he was feeling. How he wanted to take Chase in his arms and comfort him. To share a moment together where there was no pain, where everything was all right and… beautiful even. When he looked up, Chase had run off, leading the way back. Nathan exhaled deeply. He'd lost his opportunity. He needed someone to talk to, to speak honestly with about his feelings and about the pressure building steadily inside him.

A WEEK had passed since the barbecue, and Chase had still not spoken with Jarod. He'd left several messages. The first had started out with apologies and an invite to get together again. On the next he went for the buddy approach and made, in retrospect, some pretty lame jokes. He paced inside the guest cottage holding his cell phone in his hand, staring at it, willing it to ring. His hurt had moved to disappointment over the summer he had hoped to experience with Jarod. And now that disappointment was transitioning into anger. Why had *he* apologized in the first place? He had nothing to be sorry for; he was just being himself, being true. Jarod was the one who had betrayed him and left him for dead on the roadside, metaphorically speaking. Chase paced more quickly around the room, balling one hand into a fist as the other dialed Jarod's number.

No surprise, it went to his voice mail. "Jarod, it's Chase. You know what? You're a coward. I'm not going to feel bad about what happened anymore. And by the way, I'm taking back my apology. I'm not sorry—you should be apologizing to me. This isn't about being gay or straight or whatever the hell you want to call yourself. This is about being a man, and being a man means protecting the people that you love, and you obviously aren't capable of that so it's not like I'd want to be with you anyway. Not that you were in love with me because you definitely… this is stupid. Have a good summer. I won't be calling again."

Chase hung up and sat on his bed. He didn't feel any better. He'd thought maybe the call would get out his anger so he could move on. Unfortunately, he still felt dumped and it sucked.

He lay back on the bed and crossed his arms behind his head, looking at the ceiling. Tyler had been spending more and more time with Bre lately, which meant their time together had been relegated to working hours at the golf course and sleeping, but that didn't count. Chase had become quite accustomed to hugging a pillow and taking solace in its feathery embrace.

It all seemed to circle back to the question of what he was doing here. He'd come to make some cash working on the golf course and to hang out with his best friend. He was banking some cash that would surely come in useful during the new school year, but beyond that he couldn't say he was having fun anymore. It had all gotten a little messy since his coming out. And the strangest element was the fact that he was feeling closer to Tyler's father lately than to Tyler. They had an easy camaraderie. Nathan made him laugh, and he felt good when they were together. It was surprisingly easy actually, and comforting, like Nathan was filling a part of Chase he hadn't known was empty.

He wanted to feel again, like on the bonfire night in the woods or in the back of the truck under the stars with Jarod.

Chase sat up on his bed with a new resolve. He wasn't going to walk around like a zombie, wishing to live, wishing to feel, wishing and waiting to be embraced by life. He was going to start embracing it and following his instincts. A tingle ran down his arms. It was scary and exciting. He'd become a master at burying his impulses, and now the opportunity to let them bubble to the surface and follow their lead brought with it a powerful feeling—confidence.

He was going to have an amazing summer ripe with life and passion. Jarod wasn't going to stop that. Chase had just pushed out of his cocoon, and he certainly had no intention of being pressured back into its confines. The world was wide and held infinite possibilities, and he intended to experience them.

Chase stood and decided his grieving period for Jarod needed to end. He was moving on, and the best way was to wash the wallowing right off. Chase stripped off his clothes and hopped in the shower, placing his face right under the faucet and enjoying the forehead massage as the water danced over his skin. Admittedly Nathan's open-concept design was a little strange when it came to the glass shower in the corner of the room, but it was also very freeing. He had nothing to hide, not anymore. Those days were over. Just then he heard the guest cottage door open, and he instinctively turned off the shower and grabbed a towel. Maybe he wasn't totally ready to be free… or at least naked with whoever had walked in.

"I forgot to tell you. My grandma invited us all over for the weekend," Tyler called out as he shut the door and crossed to the closet, pulling shirts from hangers and stuffing them into a duffel bag.

"Had my fill of social gatherings after the barbecue. I'll just stick around here," Chase answered, briskly drying himself off and then wrapping the towel around his waist.

"So… what? You're suddenly scared to be naked in front of a heterosexual?" Tyler asked, turning with one eyebrow cocked quizzically.

"Whatever, dude. I'm not scared," Chase said, tightening the towel.

"Why are you being so prissy with that towel, then?"

"Why are you watching how I dry myself?" Chase shot back.

"Well, usually you parade around, jingling your jangles all over the place. It's hard *not* to get an eyeful." Tyler turned and grabbed a pair of cargo shorts from the shelf.

"Is it different now? Between us?" Chase asked, already sensing the answer.

"No, I'm just saying.. well, just thinking of all the times before when...."

"So, it is different."

"Kinda," Tyler said, looking at Chase with a slight shrug.

Chase watched his friend as he turned away and went back to gathering things for his weekend trip. It wasn't supposed to change. It wasn't supposed to be any different. He took a deep breath and pulled the towel from around his waist, shaking his hips. "Sorry to interrupt your programming, the show's back on schedule!"

Tyler glanced over and then pulled his hand over his eyes. "I didn't say I wanted the show back on! I still have the reruns playing in my head!"

"No, you want it, you got it, pally."

"I don't want it! I want it to stop! I was just pointing out the difference!" Tyler laughed. "I like the difference!"

"You're getting a parade," Chase threatened, running at Tyler and flicking the towel at him. "Rain or shine!"

"I don't want the parade!" Tyler said, this time seriously, and zipped up his duffel bag. "You're free to jangle all over the place for the weekend—I'm out of here."

TYLER TOSSED his duffel bag in his mom's Land Rover and headed into the house to tell his dad they were headed out. He planned on extending his usual offer to see if his dad would be joining them at his grandmother's for the weekend and was expecting the usual answer. His dad never attended functions at his mother-in-law's house; the woman seemed to stretch his patience over the course of a dinner, so Tyler couldn't even imagine them together over a whole weekend.

Tyler found his dad sitting at the dining room table, coffee in hand and reading the newspaper. "Sure you don't want to come?"

"Positive," he said without looking up from his headlines. "I'm happy as a clam right here."

Tyler pulled something from the back pocket of his jeans and tossed it on the table. "Look what I found in the guest cottage. A super old photo of you."

Nathan picked up the photo and grimaced. "It's not super old."

"Kinda looks like me."

His father examined the photo of himself in his old football uniform more closely. "It looks a lot like you. I still feel that young, you know. You feel the same on the inside. It's just the package that changes."

"Yeah, well, yours changed a lot. You used to be a stud, Dad," Tyler joked, punching his dad in the arm as a farewell gesture.

"Watch out. It'll happen to you too!" Nathan called after him, his eyes still on the photo.

"Chase is gonna be here too…," Tyler said, poking his head back in the dining room as his mother and Birdy rolled their suitcases down the hall.

"Tyler, would you take these to the car, please?" his mother asked, handing her bag over. "Make sure Chase gets something to eat once in a while, okay, Nathan? Don't leave him stranded out there. Make sure he feels comfortable enough to come in the house to get whatever he wants."

"Yeah, right, of course," he assured her and stood to give them hugs as they went out the door.

LESS THAN five minutes had passed on the drive when Birdy interrupted the silence. "What does gay mean?"

Tyler's mom turned around from the front passenger seat to lower her sunglasses in her daughter's direction. "Who told you that word?"

Tyler rapped his fingers against the steering wheel. "It's not a bad word, Mom."

"I never said it was. I asked where she heard it," she said defensively.

"Brian said he thinks Tyler and Chase are gay," Birdy stated matter-of-factly.

Tyler's drumming grew to an agitated staccato beat. "What does Brian know? He's, like, ten."

"I'm ten," Birdy replied, as if this piece of information validated both herself and her informant as forces to be reckoned with.

"I know, Birdy," Tyler conceded. His sister was indeed wise beyond her years. "Look, gay isn't a bad thing."

"So, what is it?"

She obviously wasn't going to give up, and so Tyler began to formulate the best explanation he could muster. "Birdy, sometimes a guy will fall in love with another guy. Or a girl will fall in love with a girl. That means they're gay."

"Okay."

72

The reply seemed satisfied, succinct. Maybe, just maybe, this would be the end of her questioning. Tyler wished it both for himself and for his mother, who was now massaging her temples. No such luck.

"I love Jenna, my tennis coach. Am I gay?" Birdy asked.

Tyler and his mother turned to answer Birdy simultaneously, although their answers probably only proved to confuse her further.

"No!" their mother said curtly.

"You might be," Tyler suggested cautiously.

His mom glared at him. "But you probably aren't."

"It has to do with love and… and other stuff, Birdy…." Tyler began his explanation again.

"Like sex?"

Their mother went back to massaging her temples, defeated. "Oh Lord…."

"It's okay, Mom, I know. Jeffrey told me all about it," Birdy assured her mother.

"Of course he did…."

Birdy stared out the window for a few blessed moments of silence, moments when Tyler again silently willed his sister's curiosity to be quelled. It wasn't.

"But how do two boys do that?" she asked. Tyler imagined the gears in her mind spinning.

His mother pulled off her sunglasses and turned to fully face her daughter to emphasize the importance of her new game plan. "Remember our rule to not talk about golf? I'm changing that. We can all talk about golf, especially this weekend with your grandmother. And after the weekend, Birdy, we're both going to learn how to play."

Tyler smirked to himself as he pulled the Land Rover onto the highway. "Yeah, Mom… there's nothing straighter than a couple of lady golfers."

GRANDMA WAS already pouring the early afternoon wine when they arrived and gathered around a table drenched in linen. The little tea party was missing tea but benefited from sitting in the shade of a massive weeping willow whose sloth-like branches hung clear down to the lawn.

Birdy unfolded one of the crisp serviettes from the table and laid it ladylike on her lap. "Grandma, I saw Jeffrey's penis!"

Grandma continued to pour and turned to verify with Stacey, in all

73

sincerity, "No wine for her, right?"

"She's ten, Mother," Stacey responded, taking a healthy gulp of her own, sure she'd need a little buzz to get through the afternoon.

Grandma lifted her hand in the air defensively toward Stacey as if her hospitality were under attack. "I was just checking." She turned to Birdy and passed a tray of sugar cookies to the girl with a smile. "They're weird-looking, aren't they, Birdy?"

"It looked squishy," Birdy said, taking two cookies from the tray.

"Sometimes they are…."

"Mom! Please!" Stacey shot her mother a look of outrage.

"Well, she's bound to find out one day. There's nothing wrong with a little education. More wine, dear?" Grandma asked, already uncorking a second bottle.

"Yes, please."

"Tyler?" Grandma offered, already filling a glass for her grandson.

"Tyler doesn't drink wine," Stacey said, pulling the glass from her lips.

"Of course he doesn't," Grandma assured her as she handed the nearly overflowing crystal to Tyler. "So where is Nathan?"

"He had to stay back," Stacey lied, knowing full well she was incapable of doing a convincing job of it to her mother. "He had some…"

"…work. Of course." Grandma finally took her seat, emitting an exasperated breath as if this concern had been plaguing her all day. "I don't know why he's scared of me. It's not like I'd say anything we don't already know."

"Mom…," Stacey cautioned, shooting a glance at Tyler and Birdy.

Grandma rolled the stem of her crystal between her thumb and fingers gingerly. "Well, not to his face. That might upset him."

NATHAN PUSHED his glass under the ice maker, listening to the freezer drawer rattle as it dispensed the cubes. He opened the fridge and poured a tall glass of iced tea. He noticed Chase setting up his easel in the backyard as he stirred in sugar. Nathan pulled another glass from the cupboard and filled it, watching as Chase turned, taking in the panoramic view of the lake, probably deciding on what should fill his blank canvas.

Nathan had considered many options upon hearing he and Chase would be alone for the weekend. He'd flirted with the idea of going to Stacey's mother's house to avoid a moment precisely like this. At the same time, it was exactly a moment like this that he longed for. Just to watch and admire the handsome guy through a pane of glass. Nathan measured out two teaspoons of sugar and stirred them into Chase's glass, glancing between the mesmerizing dissolving crystals and Chase removing his T-shirt and hooking it into a belt loop on his jeans. He took a deep breath, picked up the drinks, and headed out to the backyard.

"Thirsty?" Nathan asked, raising the glasses for Chase to see as he crossed the lawn.

"Nice. Yeah, that's great, thanks!" Chase smiled, resting his hands on his hips. "I haven't even started yet and you're calling break time!"

"Didn't mean to interrupt," Nathan apologized, handing Chase his iced tea.

"It's all good. I've been trying to decide what to focus on anyway. Not much of a…."

"Landscape guy," Nathan finished for him.

"You were listening." Chase smiled and his eyes twinkled dangerously at Nathan over his glass. "Are you busy right now?"

"Not really, what do you need?"

"Sit for me," Chase half asked, and half instructed.

"What?"

"Well, if you're not busy, you can be my subject. Like you said, I paint people, not scenery."

"I don't know… I mean, what do I have to do?" Nathan asked, already starting to sweat.

"Nothing. Just be. It's easy on your end. I do all the work, I promise," Chase said, picking up his easel. "Come on, I have a perfect spot."

Nathan followed Chase, who led him down the winding rock stairway off the cliff toward the lake. He sensed that Chase had his mind made up and wasn't going to be taking no for an answer. The little roller coaster started down near his groin again and began doing loops into his stomach and chest as he hurriedly followed Chase down the steps. He muffled a laugh, realizing that more than a small part of him couldn't wait to get started too.

"Down here, on the dock," Chase called over his shoulder, and now Nathan was only a moment behind. "I painted a little boy fishing down here. And now—we find the little boy in you." Chase grinned, looking enamored with his idea.

Nathan followed Chase onto the rickety dock, which swayed slightly in the water and creaked under their weight. "Now what?" he asked, feeling very self-conscious.

"Just get comfortable. Take a seat and I'll get set up."

Nathan crouched down on the pier and settled into a somewhat awkward cross-legged position and wrung his hands as he watched Chase prepare. Chase unrolled a long black canvas pouch full of brushes and selected five of varying lengths and widths, stuffing them bristle up in the front pocket of his tattered and paint-smeared jeans. Nathan's eyes traced the curve of the denim as Chase crouched and rummaged through a second canvas bag of oil paints and then squeezed various colors onto his palette. The frayed bottoms of the jeans hung long over his tan feet and rested under his heels as he went about his task, mixing the colors with a knife. The roller coaster did a triple loop at the sight of Chase's bare feet. There was something erotic about seeing him mucking around the yard shirtless and shoeless, like a bohemian Huckleberry Finn.

Chase looked up at Nathan and grinned. "The light is beautiful right now. It's playing nicely on the lake behind you." He fished one of the brushes out of his pocket and dipped it in color.

Nathan wasn't sure if he was breathing. He didn't know what he should be doing. This wasn't like a photograph. A photo was over in a matter of seconds. He wasn't sure how long this was supposed to take and was feeling more and more uncomfortable by the second as Chase examined him from over the canvas wall. He couldn't read Chase's face; his eyes just seemed so intense as he worked. After a few minutes, Chase bit the paintbrush and ran a hand through his hair.

"Let's try something," he mumbled around the brush, and walked over to Nathan. "I don't think this is you, sitting this way, I mean."

Nathan struggled to untangle his legs and try something else. He had to agree; his legs already felt as if they were well on their way to falling asleep. "Should I stand?"

"Umm… I don't think so," Chase said, biting his lower lip as he considered. "Take off your shoes."

Nathan did as he was instructed, and Chase scooped them up and set them to the side. Nathan wiggled his toes in the warm air and smiled at the unexpected turn the afternoon had taken.

"I want you to imagine that you are seven years old. Your life is completely an open slate, a blank canvas. You don't worry about tomorrow and you barely recall yesterday. You are fascinated only by this moment, what is happening to you and around you right now," Chase said, bending down in front of Nathan. "Do you mind?"

Nathan shook his head. He didn't know what he was agreeing to, but he didn't care. Chase took Nathan's pant legs and pushed them up, rolling the cuff up to just below the knee. Before he knew it had happened, Chase had deftly reached in and undone the top two buttons on his shirt, leaving it hanging open, and returned to his spot behind the canvas.

"Now, just relax. Just be, do whatever you feel like. Whatever comes into your mind," Chase instructed, once again taking up his brush.

Whatever comes into my mind. He took a few deep breaths and stared out into the thick patch of lily pads and cattails a stone's throw from the dock. It was easier to focus his attention on anything other than Chase. As he sat there, he began to notice things. Details began to jump out at him as he simply observed his surroundings. He noticed the beautiful pink and yellow blossoms growing courageously in the thatch of lily pads. He traced his finger along the grain patterns in the dock, now gray with weather and age. And as he took another breath, he smelled summer—really inhaled the scent of summer for the first time since… since he couldn't remember when. He breathed in deeply the scent of sunshine dancing on his face, of the warm breeze off the lake, and of the bright blue sky.

He wiggled his toes again and smiled, seeing the sunshine gliding between them. He wanted to put his feet in the water… and so he did. Nathan swayed his legs back and forth, and the cool water swirled in little whirlpools around them. He watched the little water cyclones, mesmerized by their force and design. He felt overwhelmed. Overwhelmed by the simplicity of this, of all these beautiful details that had become like Monet brushstrokes in his life. He had stopped noticing the little things, and his life had become a smear of color, action, and events. He wanted to find the wonder again, the wonder in each moment, like the tender pink of the lily pad's blossom and the swirl of the whirlpool.

Nathan leaned back and lay on the dock, resting his arms behind his head. The sun's rays licked gently at his face as he continued to sway his legs back and forth in the water, and for the first time in a very long time he knew he was truly… happy.

CHASE PUT the brush in his mouth and used his thumb to smear the paint in just the right way. He looked at his work and admired it, wiping his hands on the old T-shirt hooked into his belt loop. Nathan had fallen fast asleep; his legs having stopped swaying in the water and now hanging perfectly still. Chase smiled to himself as he imagined Nathan's toes as unwilling bait for the fish meandering under the dock. He pulled the T-shirt out of his belt loop and did a general clean of his brushes, squeezing the excess paint out of the bristles and onto the fabric. He had dozens of shirts like this, and he still got a quiet thrill from destroying them with his art. The color splotches became memory triggers for pieces he had worked on. He smiled as he thought of one day in the future remembering this moment while he squeezed out the robin's-egg blue of Nathan's shirt. He glanced from his painting to the man, sleeping so soundly you'd think he'd been deprived of it for years. A sleeping giant, and Chase had proudly captured his innocence and something childlike in his friend's father.

Chase wondered what was really going on with Nathan. It seemed he was always on the verge of saying something but was censoring himself. And since Chase had come out, there was nervousness in their interactions, a restrained and cautious nature. He wondered now if his coming here this summer had less to do with himself and much more to do with someone else.

He was glad Nathan had fallen asleep as he painted. It was much easier to take in his handsome features without worrying his glances were overstaying their welcome. It was intoxicatingly interesting to devour the details of a man up close. Nathan was certainly no boy, although that was the essence of what Chase was trying to capture. The differences between Nathan and Tyler had become apparent in this little afternoon study. Nathan was solidly built, exuded confidence—he'd earned his stripes. He was seasoned by experience, disappointment, and success, and resonated with the loving attributes of a father.

Chase couldn't exactly put it into words, but his heart went out to Nathan. Chase felt something; he just wasn't sure what it was. There was no denying that Nathan was an extremely attractive man, but Chase wasn't allowing his mind to wander in that direction, at least not for any prolonged amount of time, before reining it back in and chastising himself. The feeling was more… a longing. He longed to be near the man and to be held by him and to lay his head on his chest.

Chase shook his head and dismissed the idea as he rolled up his canvas bag of brushes. He was being ridiculous. He was just lonely. He wasn't longing for Nathan; he was longing for him to be happy. That was it. What he was feeling was empathy. The lightbulb clicked on in Chase's mind. Maybe he and Nathan were the same, and the nervous tension between them was simply a longing on both their parts to tell the truth. He needed to let Nathan know he could trust him, that he was there to listen, that living with a secret like this was no way to live.

And if he was wrong… in that case he'd probably lose the closest thing to a father figure he'd had in years. He wasn't sure if he was willing to take that risk, not when they were just coming into a really cool friendship. It seemed strange that he should think the world of Tyler, as if the sun rose and set with him, and then meet his father and feel like he made Tyler appear… well, a boy in comparison.

It wasn't up to him to suggest anything to Nathan. If he had something to say, surely, he'd say it. And Chase would be there to listen and accept it, whatever it might be….

As Chase picked up the canvas and easel, his mind sifted through thoughts of Tyler. He wasn't sure how he would explain what was going on between Nathan and himself. Not that there was anything going on; it was just a friendship. Tyler probably wouldn't even ask. He'd probably sigh in relief to realize that at least he hadn't brought his friend all this way to hang out alone while he was free to fritter the nights away with Bre, even if the person his friend was hanging out with was his father.

Chase turned to attempt a silent escape up the cliff stairs so as not to disturb Nathan's afternoon dreaming, but the dock creaked under his shifting weight, and he heard a contented yawn behind him. "Hey, Chase," Nathan said dreamily. "You all finished? Can I see it?"

Chase turned and set the easel back down. "I didn't want to wake you, you looked so…."

"Tired?"

"No, peaceful," Chase responded, as Nathan stretched and leaned up on one elbow.

"So, can I see the master's work?" Nathan asked with a grin. "Or did my snoring interrupt your concentration?"

"You can see it," Chase agreed, turning the canvas toward Nathan. "It's not completely done. I still have a few things to touch up."

"Airbrushing me, huh?" Nathan joked, but his voice fell silent as he took in the painting.

"Not you, just the background, the lake and dock and stuff. Those will always be there to capture. I had to concentrate on getting you right while I had you still in one place."

"Chase, it's really good," Nathan said, smiling. "You actually made me look handsome and somehow… young."

Chase laughed. "I didn't make you look that way. I just painted what I saw."

Nathan smiled and looked down at the dock, tracing his finger along the grain of the weathered wood. "So, you headed up now?"

"Yeah. Thought I'd clean up and then… well, that's about as far as I planned." Chase laughed again, taking up the canvas and easel in his hand. "You?"

"I think I'm going to continue being a seven-year-old for a while. It's very relaxing."

"It suits you," Chase said and turned to head up the stairs.

"Hey, Chase, you want to do dinner tonight?" Nathan called. "I can't cook like Stacey, but I can barbecue."

"Barbecue sounds good."

"Say eight o'clock?"

"See you then," Chase agreed and headed up the cliff to the guest cottage, wondering how many hours lay between now and eight o'clock. However many there were, he guessed they likely wouldn't pass quickly enough.

NATHAN STOOD with a beer, looking out over the lake from the patio. He'd spent the afternoon strategizing, obsessing, and second-guessing in a continual cycle. He was going to tell him. Obviously, Chase felt something too, otherwise why would he be spending time with an older man like himself? Nathan would find the right moment and say… what exactly? He wasn't even sure where to start, and that was where the second-guessing reared its ugly head and unraveled all of the strategizing he'd painstakingly plotted. And beyond that, what was he actually hoping might happen?

Their scheduled dinner loomed ahead of him like an albatross. He shook his head in disgust as he scanned the table. A bottle of wine, candles…. His heart started beating somewhere up around his throat and his stomach turned as he realized how delusional he had become. He glanced at his watch—seven forty-five. Without another moment wasted, he quickly stripped the table of the wine and candles and returned them to the kitchen, opting for another beer for Chase and himself.

Returning outside to the patio, he took a deep pull on his beer before lighting the barbecue. He was going to need the liquid courage to get through the evening. When he turned from the grill, Chase was standing by the table, a bottle of wine in his hand.

"Thought maybe you could use some help, so I'm a little early."

"I was just about to throw the steaks on," Nathan said, his pulse racing.

"I brought some wine. I didn't know what we were eating, so I brought red. Guess that works, right?" Chase asked, setting the bottle on the table and noticing the beer. "Or beer works too. I wasn't sure, but I wanted to bring something."

"Well, you can take your pick," Nathan offered.

"I'll take the beer. To be honest, I haven't really grown into liking wine yet. I think it's something that comes with age."

Nathan uncapped the beer for Chase and handed it to him. "That's what they say, you know. It gets better with time. The wine… and your appreciation of it too, I guess."

The men stood lost in their own thoughts momentarily. Finally, Nathan broke the silence. "Well, I should get started or we'll never get to eat." He walked past Chase into the kitchen and pulled the marinating steaks from the fridge, taking a deep breath as he pushed its door closed with his knee. *Keep it together*, he commanded himself before returning to the patio.

Chase was leaning with his back against the patio railing and seemed to be studying Nathan as he returned to the barbecue and forked the meat onto the grill.

"Why so serious?" Nathan asked, taking up the brush and basting the steaks with the marinade.

Chase shook his head and looked up at Nathan incredulously. "You're really strong, you know that?"

"What do you mean?"

"It's just...," Chase started, then seemed to think better of it. "It's nothing."

"No, really. What is it?" Nathan asked, glancing over at Chase.

"Well, to live this life—your life," Chase finally said.

Nathan turned and stared at him. He could hardly believe Chase was being so straightforward and that the elephant in the room was being acknowledged before they even sat down to dinner. He swallowed hard and shook his head, returning his focus to the steaks. "It's just life. I don't think it's that courageous."

"I can't imagine it."

"Things were different twenty years ago, Chase."

"That's exactly what I mean. I think it's easier to be yourself now. Like for me, sure it's hard, but I kind of take it for granted that I can be who I want to be."

Nathan closed the barbecue lid, walked over to the patio railing, and stared out over the lake. He wasn't sure how to start and wasn't even sure if he should. The last thing he felt was any sense of control right now. He certainly hadn't expected Chase to broach the subject. His fists clenched around the ornate metal railing as if to steady himself against the flow of thoughts all but ready to burst out of him. "When Tyler told me about you...," he began and then stopped, his mouth dry from the anxiety. Nathan took a swig of his beer and began again slowly, deliberately crafting each sentence. "I can't stop thinking about it. I don't want to think about it."

Nathan turned from the lake, and his gaze danced around Chase's face, unable to hold his eyes for any length of time. "It's just that all this—" He gestured lazily around the yard and almost with an air of defeat toward the cabin. "—none of it seems real anymore. Your life is going to be so... free."

Nathan's eyes finally met Chase's, and volumes were spoken in the momentary silence. Nathan let out a little laugh, but it was more shock than anything. He brought his fist to his mouth, terrified. "I've got to stop talking. I think you should go."

Chase blanched and he recoiled slightly like a twice-shy dog. Then, as if gathering his courage, he took a deep breath and stepped closer to Nathan, placing a gentle hand on his shoulder.

Now it was Nathan who shrank under the touch, letting Chase's hand fall from his shoulder and keeping his eyes trained on the ground. "Chase... I... I really think you should go."

Nathan couldn't see what was happening on Chase's face, nor did he want to. The best he could manage right now was to not fall over. He was suddenly feeling very nauseous. He watched the white sneakers turn, pause for a moment, and then quickly walk away.

CHASE NEARLY tripped as he ran across the yard to the guest cottage. He was now more sure than ever of what was really going on with Nathan, and yet at the same time terrified he had pushed too hard to uncover the truth. He'd only wanted to offer comfort, and Nathan had pushed him out. Chase opened the door and crossed to his bed, slumping down onto it and driving the palms of his hands into his forehead in frustration. Clearly the last thing the man needed was a fledgling and fumbling gay trying to drag him out of the closet. If he was even in the closet. Maybe he wasn't gay. When Chase considered it, there was very little evidence to state his case and yet there was this… feeling. Something in the way their eyes met that informed Chase he wasn't chasing some wild hypothesis.

Chase rolled over and opened the bedside table drawer where he kept his art supplies. He reached in, set the rolled-up canvas bags of brushes and knives aside, and searched for the photo he had been keeping there. He liked to look at it from time to time and imagine what his own father might have looked like in a photograph from that era. Would he have resembled his father at this age as much as Tyler did Nathan? It was also fun to create an idea of what Nathan's life might have been like at this age. The stud football player all grown up into a family man. It was difficult to imagine Nathan without the distinguished air that now seemed to emanate from him. Chase scoured the wooden drawer's bottom, but his hand came out empty. The photo was gone.

NATHAN SAT in one of the two lawn chairs perched on the roof of the cabin. He wasn't sure how long he'd been roosting up here, only that the sun had now sunk into the other side of the lake and the stars had taken up their residence in the crepuscular sky. He had watched as the orbs of light appeared one by one, marveling at the vastness of it all and wondering why the struggle within him could feel so monumental when his life was but a flickering glimmer compared to these heavenly bodies. He felt a responsibility to his family, that was certain, but he also felt a responsibility to himself. He had never mistrusted his attraction to other men, nor had he ever been plagued by a belief that there was anything intrinsically immoral or base about his nature. He believed his union with Stacey and the timing of their pregnancy must have been destined for him, as surely as the stars seemed to hold their fixed positions in the sky. He was meant to be a father, and so he embraced the responsibility and stopped questioning it a long time ago. But now... now he wondered if there wasn't a new destiny awaiting him, one that would require him to stop denying his true nature and embrace his authentic self. He turned to look over at the guest cottage and saw the light in the windows there dim until every pane of glass was a dark mirror reflecting the yard. The question, which still pierced his mind, was: could he hang on to his family and himself?

STACEY HELD the rose-petaled teacup between her hands tightly, channeling comfort through its warmth. Tyler and Birdy were busy occupying themselves in their grandma's garden shed constructing a birdhouse. Stacey was pleased that despite their age gap the two got on well, perhaps due more to Birdy's maturity than to Tyler's. She hummed to herself as she surveyed her mother's yard, a venerable mosaic of color. It was a wonder she was so capable of such orchestrated botany in light of her habit of starting happy hour around noon. *Maybe she gardens in the morning*, Stacey mused.

"Brandy, darling?"

Stacey turned to see her mother crossing the yard with a crystal decanter, dressed for an Easter parade in bonnet and pearls. "I have tea, thank you."

"I know, dear. That's what I meant, brandy for your tea?" she asked, uncorking the decanter, ready to pour.

"I'm fine, thank you. You go ahead," Stacey said, turning back to admiring the sprays of color in the garden.

"You know I never really started drinking until your father passed," she explained, filling her teacup with amber. She poured out a splash from the crystal on the lawn. "God rest his soul."

Her mother settled into the chair beside Stacey and joined her in audience of the yard. "I'm worried about you, Stacey."

"Why? There's nothing to worry about."

"Of course there is. The children are growing up. You need to find a hobby to occupy your time. Stillness will make you crazy."

"I'm fine, really, Mom."

Her mother raised an eyebrow skeptically. "Have you and Nathan talked about… you know?"

"He'll bring it up when he's ready. It's not my place," Stacey answered, wiping a stray tress of hair away from her forehead. "Besides, maybe there's nothing to discuss."

"Stacey…." Her mother reprimanded her in a single word. "All I'm suggesting is that you're still young, you have a lot of years ahead of you…."

"I love him, Mom," Stacey said, shaking her head. "Nothing changes that."

After that it seemed there was little left to say. The ladies sipped their tea and feigned excited interest as Tyler and Birdy emerged from the garden shed with their little cedar birdhouse and animatedly discussed where the most perfect spot for it in the yard might be. Stacey contemplated her situation. She couldn't force her husband into a confession he wasn't yet willing to make, but perhaps she could find an innocent way to prod him along.

LATE THE next afternoon, Chase was stooped over, rummaging around in the fridge, when Nathan walked into the kitchen. "I was, uh, I was just going to make a sandwich or something. You want one?"

The look on Nathan's face when Chase looked up was a delicate mixture of trepidation and determination. He closed the fridge and stood in silence, not wanting to distract the man from his mission. Nathan took a step closer, and his eyes flickered with fear before meeting Chase's steadily as if searching for his courage within them. "Chase, I...," he started and then paused, looking away as if the words had scurried into the kitchen corner and he had to retrieve them before starting again. "I think that I...."

Chase stepped closer and laid a comforting hand on his shoulder. This time the touch seemed to hit its mark, and Nathan did not shrink away from it. "It's okay. I know." His words seemed to lift a giant weight from Nathan's shoulders. "It's all right. Everything's going to be all right."

Nathan stepped closer, his hulking shoulders slumped like those of a little boy who'd been chastised, and Chase drew him into a hug. They stood there in an embrace and protected each other against the world and all the discomforts that existed outside of the little sanctuary they had created in this kitchen. He wasn't sure what more words of comfort he could offer or how to proceed, and so he remained as he was, holding the man in silence.

It was Nathan who spoke first. "I've never been with...."

"Shhh... it's okay." The words lilted out of Chase like a lullaby as he gently rubbed Nathan's back.

"I have no one else to talk to," Nathan mumbled into Chase's hair.

"Don't worry, I'm here," Chase reassured him, holding Nathan tighter.

Nathan ducked his head and looked into Chase's face, smiling a silent thanks, and then rested his forehead against Chase's. It was a bonding gesture both paternal and shockingly intimate. And then Nathan lifted his chin and met Chase's lips. Gently and so tentatively that Chase barely registered it at first with his eyes pressed closed.

It was an invitation.

Chase opened his eyes and pulled back in surprise. That he might act as a companion and comfort, sure. But that Nathan would be thinking of him romantically had not entered into the realm of possibilities.

And yet... and yet as he looked at the man he knew instinctively that Nathan embodied what he was searching for. The attraction had been palpable since they'd first met. And now here were the seasoned, handsome features he found so desirable in his best friend… a torturous infatuation that would never be reciprocated. And a man capable of bestowing on him the love of a father he'd never truly known.

Chase leaned in and kissed Nathan, a cautious signal that the gesture was accepted. It was fragile and perfect. The men pulled apart and spoke volumes with their eyes, each checking, reassuring, and double-checking as they used restraint in exploring each other through kisses. Neither spoke, both excited by the magic they were creating and terrified any one word might dispel it.

The evening was wearing on, and twilight had gathered her cloak across the yard when Nathan reached down and took Chase's hand, leading him out of the kitchen. Chase kept his eyes fixed on Nathan's back as he followed him through the house and into a room he'd never seen. Nathan crossed to the bedside lamp and clicked it on, giving the bedroom a soft, warm glow. Chase sat down on the bed, watching and breathing in shallow gulps, his chest rising and falling under his T-shirt.

"Are you okay?" Nathan asked, sitting on the bed beside him.

"Yeah," Chase managed to get out. "Just nervous, I guess. And excited. I've never been with… well, anyone either."

Nathan smiled and took his hand, kissing it softly. "You are so handsome…."

"Look who's talking." Chase laughed nervously. "I'm not even sure what to do…."

"I'm sure we'll figure it out," Nathan replied as he leaned in and kissed Chase's neck.

Chase thrilled at the feeling of Nathan's stubble grazing his chin, at the scent of him this close, and at how his large hand wrapped effortlessly around his own. Soon Nathan had slipped one of his hands up Chase's shirt and was exploring his skin. Chase reached out and timidly began to undo the buttons on Nathan's shirt, slipping his hand inside. Nathan's chest was so warm, and he could feel the other man's heart beating thunderously under the palm of his hand. Chase turned his mouth to meet Nathan's. The kiss was ravenous, as if Nathan were the food he'd been craving after a famine. He only pulled his mouth away long enough to stand and let Nathan pull the T-shirt up and over his head.

Chase tore through the remaining buttons on Nathan's shirt and pulled it off his shoulders before pushing him down on the bed and falling on top of him. His breath caught in his throat at the sensation of their bodies colliding, skin against skin. They groped and grabbed each other in a violent and desperate attempt to express a lifetime of repressed yearning.

It was more than Chase had ever expected: more liberating, more erotic, more exquisitely brutal and viciously loving than anything he'd ever encountered. And when they had finished, they lay contented in each other's arms, breathing heavily and desperate to remain undivided.

"You know, you look pretty good in my shirt," Nathan commented, leaning the carton of strawberry ice cream back toward Chase.

Chase dug his spoon in, retrieving a mountainous pink heap. "And you look pretty good without it." He grinned, bumping his shoulder playfully against Nathan's. Chase had pulled on Nathan's button-down shirt and was marveling at how the 2XL swam on him. They sat in reckless abandon together on the couch in their boxer shorts, as if the lake house were a secluded honeymoon suite. "So… we figured it out, huh?"

Nathan laughed and pulled Chase in closer. "I'd say so."

"You said we would," Chase agreed, cleaning his spoon.

"And now that we figured it out, we can keep practicing until we get it perfect."

"If that wasn't perfect, I don't know if I can handle what's next," Chase purred, taking the ice cream from Nathan and setting it on the living room table. He climbed on top of Nathan and began kissing his neck, his lips still chilled from the cold spoon.

"Before round two, I have an idea," Nathan suggested, his voice a low enticing rumble. "Want to take a swim?"

Red and white Chinese lanterns cast a warm glow across the glassy surface of the lake as Chase and Nathan slipped out of their shorts on the creaking dock and jumped in. The chilly water was a shock to their naked skin, and they were soon treading water and clinging to each other to stay warm. Nathan was enthralled to be living so dangerously, completely infatuated with Chase and the new life he represented. He reached out and traced his fingers along Chase's jawline, pulling him in closer. "It's amazing…."

Nathan petted Chase's lips with his thumb, marveling at their fullness. "I've been dreaming about a moment like this all my life, but I never thought it might actually happen."

Chase smiled coyly. "Well, was it worth the wait?"

Nathan nodded with a smile and pulled Chase into another kiss. Moonlight cut across the lake as they turned around each other in the water, savoring the serenity of being together, the safety of their privacy and the protection it provided from the big wide world that would say this was wrong.

Slam!

They turned abruptly to look up toward the cabin, hearing a car's doors being pushed shut, the echo cutting clear down to the lake.

"Shit. Somebody's here," Nathan uttered nervously and began to swim for the dock. After pulling himself onto it, he grabbed his clothes and ran up to the cabin without another look back at Chase.

STACEY, TYLER, and Birdy pulled their suitcases out of the car and dragged them into the lake house. The trip had exhausted Stacey. More specifically, her mother had exhausted her, and she was quite ready to sink into the comfort of her own home.

"Birdy, start unpacking your things, please, and I'll be in to help you in a minute," she said, already heading through the living room to her own bedroom. She glanced at the carton of ice cream on the table and shook her head; it had begun to melt out of the bottom of the box. Noting the second spoon, she smiled to herself. At least Nathan had taken her advice and fed the boy, albeit perhaps not what she would have chosen.

Stacey set her suitcase on the bed and began unpacking just as Nathan emerged from their washroom with a towel around his waist and another drying his hair. "You're back early."

"I love my mother, but three days would be pushing it." She leaned in for a kiss, resting her hand on his chest. "You're shivering… out of hot water?"

"Yeah… I'll have to check the pilot light on the hot-water tank," he said, tossing the towels in the laundry hamper and pulling on a dry shirt and some sweatpants.

"I saw you fed Chase," Stacey remarked, hanging her clothes back in the closet.

Nathan turned to her with a startled expression.

"The ice cream? I hope there was more to the meal than just dessert," she scolded playfully. "It's melting right now in the living room."

"Oh geez… I completely forgot. I'll clean it up," Nathan apologized and hurried out of the room.

CHASE SHIVERED in the cold water, not sure what to do next. Nathan had not returned, and he was about to head for the dock when he heard someone scrambling down the cliff stairs. Nathan must have dealt with whoever had stopped by. He smiled, anticipating an opportunity to resume where he and Nathan had left off by suggesting a hot shower.

His smile quickly faded as Tyler ran yelling onto the dock, pulling off his shirt and shoes and diving into the water. He emerged ten feet in front of Chase in the dark water and swam toward him. "Hey."

Chase swallowed hard and tried to gather his thoughts. Reality was crashing down hard all around him. "Hey."

"Night swim, huh?" Tyler exclaimed with a splash. "Love coming out for a night swim. It's gorgeous out here, right?"

"Yeah… totally." Chase nodded, unable to completely look at his friend.

"So, how did it go hanging with the old man?"

"It was all right."

"Lots of golf talk probably," Tyler guessed and leaned back floating, taking in the starry sky. "You missed out at my grandma's place. Happy hour starts at breakfast. There were mimosas at nine, wine by eleven."

Chase tried to casually lean back and join Tyler in floating, taking in the night sky, but the guilt was nearly pulling him under.

"Oh God! Put that thing away!" Tyler exclaimed. "I can see your jangler floating. Way to wreck a perfect view!"

Chase sank back into the water, having forgotten his shorts were lying abandoned on the dock.

"Aren't you scared a fish is gonna bite that worm off?" Tyler joked, pushing Chase's head down under the water.

Chase emerged and splashed Tyler. Maybe if he pretended like nothing was amiss, that nothing had changed, then he could make the weekend disappear and everything would return to normal. He yelled and swam after Tyler, putting him in a headlock.

"Ahhh! Get away from me," Tyler screamed, pushing Chase away. "I felt your jangler jingle against my leg! Come on, I'll race you in. It's freezing out here. You're gonna get frostbite."

Tyler turned with a splash and swam to the dock. The regret grew in Chase's stomach like a lead weight, threatening to drag him down into the lake. His arms and legs felt weak, and he knew he had to swim to shore now or his remorse would surely swallow him alive. "Oh God, what did I do," he whispered.

CHASE HAD risen early, still unable to quiet his mind after a sleepless night. He was determined to tell Nathan that what had happened was a mistake. It had obviously been completely irrational, and it couldn't continue. They had nearly been caught, and he was sure the consequences of that wouldn't be lost on Nathan.

Chase swung his legs out of bed and pulled on some shorts, a tank top, and his running shoes. Hopefully he could run the anxiety away and exhaust himself to the point of being able to sleep the following night. He knew that once he'd had an opportunity to have a levelheaded conversation with Nathan in the light of day, everything would be put into perspective.

Chase looked over at Tyler, still sound asleep, the covers pulled over his head. He slipped out of the guest cottage silently and crossed the still-dewy grass to the cliff stairs overlooking the lake. Perhaps stretching out on the dock and revisiting the last spot he and Nathan had shared a moment would chase away any lingering shadows from the previous night.

The crisp morning air felt good in his lungs, and his head was beginning to clear as he jogged down the stairs. Seeing he wasn't alone, he stopped in his tracks and was about to attempt a silent retreat when he was spotted from the dock.

"Oh, Chase! Good morning, come here a minute," Stacey called, looking up from organizing seed packages into a handcrafted wooden box.

Chase took a deep breath and jogged the last steps down the hill and out onto the pier. Stacey sat on a cedar bench in a sundress and light sweater. Steam from a coffee cup billowed out in the brisk morning air and disappeared over the lake. "You're up early," Chase stated as he approached.

"You too." Stacey set the box of seeds down and paused, collecting her thoughts before looking up again at Chase. "I wanted to talk to you about something."

Chase shifted his weight uncomfortably.

"When were you going to tell me?" she continued.

A myriad of emotions welled up inside him. "Okay, I can...."

"It's okay. I've decided I'm okay with it," Stacey continued with a reassuring smile.

"You're... okay with it...." He let the words fall from his mouth, desperately trying to chase after their significance.

She looked out over the lake and took up the coffee cup in her hands, wrapping them around the warm china. "When Nathan and I were getting married I had my… doubts. I know how you feel. I didn't think I could tell anyone at first either. I don't even know if I really loved Nathan at the time, but Tyler was already a little boy, and I couldn't have done it alone." She looked down into her cup, as if the rest of her story were written inside it. "I don't think I knew what love was… but I knew what I had to do and eventually we *grew* to love each other."

Stacey picked up the wooden box of seeds again and beckoned Chase over to take it from her. "So, I've decided I'll plant a perennial to symbolize the new you and the love that will grow inside you, stronger and stronger, year after year." She smiled at the thought. "Pick one."

Chase wasn't really sure what was happening but decided it best if he did as instructed until he could figure it out. He flipped through the seed packages quickly and selected a yellow flower, handing the package to Stacey.

"Stella de Oro daylily. Beautiful choice," she commented, tapping the package with her finger. "Each flower blooms only once and then dies. You know, I don't know why I didn't put it together sooner. I'm a little hurt that you didn't tell me, but I understand."

"Hurt that I didn't tell you…?" Chase asked, now completely at a loss.

"Of course. Birdy was the one who finally pointed it out to me. She knew right away."

Chase felt his face blanch. "Birdy knows!"

Stacey waved away his concern, "Don't worry, Birdy's fine with it. She's one hip little girl."

"Wait, Birdy knows that we…."

"That you're gay," Stacey finished for him, with a comforting smile.

"Oh, thank God." Chase sighed in relief.

"I know. It must have been terrible to feel you had to keep a secret like that. Why didn't you tell me?"

Chase looked at Stacey and decided that after all of this, she deserved the truth. "What you said at the barbecue, I didn't think you'd understand."

"Oh, with Jenna and the… oh Chase, I'm so sorry, if I'd known…." Stacey shook her head, apparently realizing her faux pas. "I hope you'll be able to forgive me. Go for your run. I'll have breakfast ready when you get back," she said, picking up the box of seeds and walking off the dock.

"Stacey?"

She turned and waited patiently.

"Thank you." Chase nodded and she smiled, returning his nod before walking up the hill.

G‍RAVEL CRUNCHED loudly under Chase's sneakers as he ran down the country road. His shirt was soaked with sweat and his lungs were screaming from the exertion. He wanted to rid himself of the iniquity that was consuming him from the inside out. Seeing Stacey and having *her* apologize to *him* had been too much. There was no way he could sit at her table and casually pretend like nothing was amiss.

The green of the forest began to swirl around him, and Chase stumbled, falling to his knees and feeling the gravel tear through skin. He was glad for it. He deserved it. The guilt continued to germinate inside him, pushing against his rib cage and up and out his throat, forcing an uncontrollable retch.

NATHAN PAUSED in the doorway to the kitchen and watched Stacey, Tyler, and Birdy sitting at the dinner table, laughing and poring over a crossword in the newspaper.

"Honestly, at this rate we'll never get to eat breakfast!" Tyler complained, leaning back in his chair with a groan.

Birdy shot a reprimanding look at her brother. "We can't eat until it's finished."

"Birdy, I have no idea. Just because I go to college doesn't make me smart."

Stacey looked up to see Nathan standing in the doorway. "Your father will probably know. Should we ask him?" she suggested, escaping to the kitchen to bring in breakfast.

Nathan gave a practiced smile as he walked in and sat at the table with his family. "Ask him what?"

"Dad! What's a ten-letter word for bond?" Birdy asked, flashing the crossword in his direction.

Nathan considered as he stirred cream into his coffee. "Hmmm… investment?"

Stacey returned with hot plates of pancakes, sausage, and eggs Benedict as Birdy tried the word in the empty boxes, her pencil dancing over the paper. "Investment doesn't work."

"Where's Chase? We're gonna be late for work," Tyler said, grabbing a sausage from the stack and taking a bite.

"Tyler, use a plate, please," Stacey said, trying to hand him one, but he waved her off, making a pancake-and-sausage sandwich and heading out the door.

"What are you doing today, Daddy?" Birdy asked, momentarily setting aside the crossword to fill her plate.

"I'm going to do some paperwork and then play a round of that game we're not allowed to mention."

The lapse in focus didn't last long as Birdy again turned to the newspaper. "I still need a ten-letter word for bond."

Nathan reflected for a second and then replied, "Try commitment."

"I've changed the rule," Stacey interrupted, finally sitting down to her own food.

"*C-O-M*—is there one *M* or two *M*s?" Birdy asked, looking up at her father.

"What's this?" Nathan asked Stacey before turning to Birdy. "There are two *M*s, kiddo...."

"*I-T-M-E-N-T,*" Birdy said, filling in the letters. "It works! You got it, Daddy!"

Stacey smiled at her daughter as she cut into her eggs Benedict. "I've changed the rule. We can all talk about golf. As much as we want."

"Golf, golf, golf... balls, balls, balls!" Birdy sang, turning her attention to the next crossword clue.

"I've been thinking, maybe it would be good for you to spend some time with Chase," Stacey suggested. "He's going through some—"

Birdy looked up suddenly and announced, "He's gay."

Nathan nodded thanks to Birdy for the information. "I know, Tyler told me."

"Did you talk to him about it?" Stacey asked between bites. "I mean, while we were away?"

Nathan pushed his food across the plate mindlessly. "A little."

"Well, I just think he could use all of our support right now," Stacey advised.

Nathan took a long sip of his coffee. "Okay, yeah, I'll talk to him."

Birdy looked back down to her crossword and contentedly sang, "Golf, golf, golf... balls, balls, balls!"

THE WEED whacker whirred as Chase worked his way around the sand trap directly behind the sixth hole. He was glad for the distraction. Between the buzzing of the gas-powered lawn groomer and the music pumping through his iPhone, he was almost able to drown out his own thoughts. He jumped when one of his earbuds was pulled out of his ear.

"Hey!" he said, spinning around, thankfully keeping the weed whacker on the ground, destroying the grass rather than his surprise assailant's face.

Nathan stood smiling with his golf bag slung over his shoulder, looking like a perfect model for an Arnold Palmer catalogue. "Where's Tyler?"

Chase pulled out his other earbud and turned off the weed whacker. "Working on the back nine. We need to talk."

Nathan gave a flirty shrug and smiled, which would have played better on a high school junior than a thirty-six-year-old. "We're talking right now."

Chase could tell this was going to be more difficult than he'd hoped. "You know what I mean."

Without another word he turned and led Nathan into the thick trees between the sixth hole and the seventh tee-off box.

STACEY LIFTED the picnic basket onto the bench between Birdy and herself. She set out a red plaid square and covered it with apple slices, two tarts, and juice boxes. The golf cart was parked a few feet away, and she waved another twosome through as they approached the tee-off box. "Go ahead, we're just taking a little break."

She inhaled deeply and looked around at the lush green of the golf course. "It is relaxing out here."

"You're not a very good golfer, Mom," Birdy observed, sticking the plastic straw in her juice box.

"Well, we're learning together, aren't we?"

Birdy grabbed an apple slice and chewed. Stacey could see that a question was forming in her young mind. "Didn't Daddy ever ask you to come play?"

"No. Sometimes even when one man and one woman are married to each other they need some time apart." Stacey reflected. "That's what golf does for your father. Well, and his car… and the office. I have my scrapping, and I love to cook."

She was surprised to hear how unconvincing the words sounded, even to her. It wasn't that she was proud of lying to her children, but she counted it as part of the multifaceted and ever-changing landscape of child rearing. It was simply a mandatory component of protecting them. At any rate Birdy was right—she wasn't a very good golfer, and she wasn't sure if it was more attributable to a lack of coordination or an unfocused mind. Her conversation with Chase this morning had instigated a flood of embarrassing recollections of unsavory comments she had made over the years about homosexuals. Not directly to them—well, at least she hoped not, but then again, she had put her foot squarely in her mouth at the barbecue with Chase and not even realized it. How many other times had she let her mouth run without considering the residual damage she might be leaving in her wake? She'd just done it again, she realized, by classifying marriage as between a man and a woman with her daughter. Evidently, she had some subconscious concerns to work out, and she decided to make a concerted effort to do so. Just then, she heard a commotion in the bushes behind them.

Stacey turned and saw two figures walking through the trees. As they came closer, she saw it was Nathan and Chase. Stacey set down her juice box and stood to call out to the men when she saw Nathan pin Chase against a tree and kiss him. Slowly she turned back to Birdy and then abruptly began to pack up the picnic basket.

"Mom! What are you doing?" Birdy complained, clearly convinced her mother was crazy.

Stacey picked up the picnic basket and covered Birdy's eyes with her other hand, leading her along to the golf cart. "It's a game. You're going to keep your eyes closed and I'll drive. When I stop, you can guess what hole we're on."

"But we're on seven. I want to play seven next!"

Stacey escorted Birdy into the passenger seat and quickly turned the keys in the ignition. "You've already called me a bad golfer today. I'm your mother. I won't also have you talking back."

Birdy craned her neck past her mother. "What were those men doing in the bushes?"

Stacey pressed the pedal to the floor and willed the golf cart to travel faster than its max speed of twenty kilometers per hour. "Probably looking for a lost ball."

NATHAN BACKED Chase up against an ancient cedar tree and leaned in for a kiss. It was all Chase could do to keep from returning it, but his mind was made up and he was on a mission. "Nathan, we can't do this."

"Of course we can," he said, running his hand up into Chase's hair and cradling his head. "I can't stop thinking about you."

Chase placed a hand on Nathan's chest and gently edged him away, looking around intently to suggest the possibility of getting caught. "I think we need to cool it. We can't just…."

The rumble of a greens tractor interrupted him, and they looked up to see Tyler sweeping the sixth green on a John Deere. Chase snuck past Nathan without another word. Their conversation would have to wait.

Chase walked up to the green, where Tyler had climbed off the tractor and was cutting around the hole with his pocketknife. Tyler cleaned the blade on his jeans and then looked up in surprise.

"Dude. Where've you been? I feel like I'm working by myself!" he said, taking a chunk of grass and chucking it at Chase.

"Been clearing brush," he said evasively. "You want to stop by the driving range after work today? I could still use a few pointers, coach."

"Can't. Bre is bringing a picnic. She's been planning it all day—"

"Why'd you bring me out here? To play board games with your

parents?" Chase interrupted, surprised at his own explosion.

Tyler stood and wiped his hands on his pants. "You're joking, right?"

"I didn't come so I could watch you go out every night with her," Chase said. He was angry with himself, but Tyler was the closest target.

"What did you come for? Sounds like you're a little jealous."

"Tyler, come on, it's not like that."

Tyler just laughed. "No, it is like that. I don't even know who you are anymore. You come here, announce that you're gay, and expect everything will be the same. It's not." Tyler turned and jumped on the tractor, leaving Chase in his dust.

STACEY SAT at the dining room table with a pinot noir, mindlessly turning the pages of a family photo album. She couldn't quite bring herself to look at the pictures and the memories that were reflected there, but it gave her something to pretend to be doing as she waited. Despite her surface stillness, a storm was heaving inside her, growing more deadly and wrathful with each passing moment. So many accusations were piling one on top of the other in her mind, she was reeling just to try keep them reined in and organized for her arsenal. It had been nearly an hour since she'd sent Birdy to play at the neighbor's house, and though she was grateful to have solitude in which to hide her grief, the waiting was nearly driving her to madness. A glass of wine to try to calm herself had turned into a near-empty bottle. The alcohol had only stirred and boiled her emotions instead of quelling them for a time as she had hoped. Hearing the front door open, she steeled herself and did not rise to meet her husband as she customarily would have, but remained seated, staring out across the table and into the yard through the large picture-frame window.

"How was your day?" she asked, impressing herself with her controlled tone.

"Good. Yours?" Nathan called from the foyer.

"Fine," Stacey said calmly before drawing her first weapon. "How's Chase?"

She could hear her husband pause in the kitchen and pull a glass from the cupboard, filling it with water. "I think he's gonna be okay."

"Mmmm...," Stacey purred, but it barely concealed the roar growing inside her throat. "And how about you? Are you going to be okay?"

Nathan set the glass on the granite countertop. "I don't know what you mean."

"Really?" she said musically, beginning to enjoy his mounting discomfort, like a cat playing with her food.

"What's this about? You told me to spend some time with Chase. What are you upset about?"

"Oh, I'm not upset," she lied, swirling the last of the pinot in her crystal, disgusted by how it reminded her of her mother. She could feel Nathan's eyes boring into her back, feel the accusation he was about to fling at her forming in his mind.

"Stacey, you're drunk."

"No, just high on the adrenaline of a good game of golf."

105

"What were you doing at the golf course?" Nathan asked, a hint of concern in his voice.

"Birdy and I went to play. I didn't realize it was out of bounds for us." She calmly closed the photo album and turned to look at him over the back of her chair. "I saw you."

It was all she could do to remain in the chair and not run over and slap him as his lying face twisted into a caricature of confusion. "Excuse me?"

"At the golf course, with Chase," she explained for his benefit. "I saw you kiss him."

And in that instant her female instincts surmised that the well was much deeper than what she had witnessed. This man whom she had shared her life with for the past twenty years could not hide the guilt that colored his face. "What else have you done?" she continued.

"Nothing....," he choked out.

"Don't lie to me, Nathan."

"This is—"

"What? Crazy? Are you about to call me crazy?" She stood and walked steadily despite the wine into the kitchen to face him. "*I am a perfectly sane woman dealing with completely irrational behavior. If you've forgotten, this is our life you're toying with. Now tell me what happened.*"

Nathan looked at the floor, shaking his head. "What you saw was an accident. It didn't mean anything."

She sneered, but the laugh in her throat started to push the tears out without her permission. "An accident is when soy sauce spills on a white shirt. An accident is forgetting to confirm dinner reservations. Cheating on your wife with a... a... I can't even say it. *That* is not an accident. When did it start?"

"Are we really going to have this conversation?"

"I *need* to know! Have you always liked... men?"

"No—yes—I don't know, Stacey."

"Considering the circumstances, I hope you can be a little more concise with your answers. Are you gay, Nathan?" she challenged.

"I don't know...."

"Yes, you do! Are you?" There was no longer any use trying to keep the storm at bay. It was a wild thing now, spilling out of her.

"Yes," he admitted, gritting his teeth against the word. "But I loved you."

"Loved," she repeated, barely able to comprehend its meaning and when it had slipped into being a thing of the past.

"You know what I mean."

She glared at him and tossed her hair back defiantly. "Actually, I don't. That's why we're having this little heart-to-heart, to raise the veil of my confusion."

He was silent for a moment. "What are you going to do?"

"You're in no position to question me. I will ask the questions. Why did you marry me?"

"We had Tyler.... I couldn't just...."

"And you knew then that you'd be living a lie?"

"This hasn't been a lie. What happened with Chase... it was the first time. I've never been with a man before."

"And so, you chose a boy. Your son's best friend to experiment with?" she spat.

"Stacey, stop, please."

"I won't stop!" she yelled, beginning to pace the kitchen. "I tried to be the perfect wife, but it didn't matter. Don't you understand? I don't care that you're gay, Nathan. I chose this life, with you, and everything that comes with it. Why didn't you just talk to me?"

"Stacey, I just couldn't—" He paused, surprise registering on his face. "If you knew all along, why didn't you just leave me?"

"Because I love you, Nathan. Because we have two children together and a home and a life, and because I thought eventually you'd tell me and I could tell you it was all right, that I didn't care, that we could keep everything we have and we could just go on—"

"Pretending," he finished for her, although the word did not give her solace or satisfaction.

She just shook her head in disgust. "But you slipped...."

"I'm sorry, it just happened. What are we going to do?"

"I don't know what *we'll* do, Nathan, but I know that *I'm* going to start by telling Chase he's leaving," she threatened, already turning on her heel.

"Stacey, don't, please. Let me handle it."

The front door opened, and silence separated them like a referee between boxers. Tyler walked into the kitchen and crossed to the fridge, stooping down to pull out a soda. "Handle what?"

Perhaps seeing that neither of his parents was inclined to answer, he continued, "What are we having for dinner?"

Stacey turned so her son wouldn't see her tear-stained cheeks. "Everyone's on their own tonight."

"Okay, I'll probably head over to Bre's, then," Tyler said, already on his way out the door.

When Tyler had left, she turned back to Nathan, who stood slumped against the kitchen counter. "Stacey, are you going to leave me?"

If her son hadn't just reminded her of her most cherished position—mother—the answer would have been easy. But as angry as she was with Nathan, her love and maternal instinct to protect her children were stronger. She needed time to absorb the implications of a choice either way. At any rate, she was not feeling generous enough to comfort Nathan with an answer to that particular question. "I think you have someone you need to have a discussion with."

She watched as Nathan nodded gravely and slinked out the door. Stacey returned to her seat at the table and stared out the picture window at the weeping willow tree framed there. She'd watched the tree grow into the towering Venus it had become. It danced a melancholy ballet now in the breeze and seemed to stretch out its hanging limbs to comfort her. It had witnessed her life as well and the growth of her family.

"Hey, Mom, have you seen Chase?"

She turned to see her son standing in the archway between the kitchen and dining room. She hoped her mask had not slipped to the point of revealing her agony. She just felt so tired, like she was at the end of a long journey, and the effort to maintain appearances at this point was beginning to feel like a trivial concern. But this was her love, this was her life, this was her child, and at all costs he had to be protected. "No, haven't seen him. I thought you were going over to see Bre."

Tyler took a seat at the table beside his mother and surveyed the empty wine bottle and family album sitting on it. "What's the matter?"

"Nothing," she lied and pulled tightly on the marionette strings that kept her mask of contented fulfillment in place. "Why would you think something's wrong?"

"Mom. I can tell." He reached out and took her hand.

She smiled, but her eyes weren't cooperating and welled slightly. "It's nothing. I just thought we could spend some time together. You've been home for a few weeks now, and I feel like we haven't even really talked."

"Yeah, I know. Guess that's part of growing up, huh?" Tyler smiled as if this piece of information might actually give her comfort. "Now you and Birdy get to spend a lot of time together."

Stacey turned her head at the mention of Birdy's name. She had no idea of how, if she had to, she would be able to explain all of this to her ten-year-old daughter. "Remember when I'd let you skip school so you could stay home and bake cookies with me?"

"Those were my favorite days."

"Or the time you were suspended in high school for a week?" she asked, smiling at the memory. "I was angry at first, but then I realized it meant we could hang out and watch movies in the afternoons. We had so much fun."

Stacey's smile was reflected on Tyler's face as they recalled a younger, more innocent time. But Tyler's eyes searched his mother's face and found what she'd hoped he would not, a chink in the armor. "Your game face doesn't work with me anymore, Mom. What's going on?"

"Nothing."

"I'm not going to leave this chair until you're straight with me."

She shook her head slightly, looking back out the window at the willow tree. "It doesn't matter, Tyler."

"Of course it does. Just talk to me," he urged, and his request reminded Stacey of her own to Nathan in the kitchen earlier. "Is it Birdy? Is it Dad? Is somebody sick?"

"No, nobody's sick," she reassured him.

"Well, then, what is it, Mom? I'm old enough. You don't need to protect me."

Stacey looked at her little boy and made the decision. She would ease his discomfort but give him no more information than was absolutely necessary. "Your dad and I are having problems. There's someone else."

TYLER OPENED the door to the guest cottage and stood there motionless, his gaze falling on Chase, who was lying on his bed and flipping through a graphic novel.

"My dad cheated on my mom. I can't believe it. What a fucking asshole," Tyler spewed, still staring at the bed and only half taking into account that Chase was there. He was processing the information as it fell from his lips. "I thought their life was so perfect, you know? I had no idea. I mean, what's he thinking, right? My mom's great. Why would he do something like that?"

Chase set the novel down and sat up on the bed. "Does she uh… does she know who he was with?"

"No." Tyler dismissed the question. "I hate him so much right now. She should leave the jerk."

"Tyler, I'm so sorry."

"I had this idea that my family was perfect. Everybody else's was falling apart but not mine. I had the TV mom and dad. I liked it that way," he said as he sank down onto his bed.

"Maybe they'll work it out," Chase suggested.

"I don't know why. It's gotta be over. Yesterday my dad was like my superhero and today he's just… shit. You're lucky you never had a dad." Tyler looked up at his friend and immediately regretted his thoughtless remark when he registered the look on Chase's face.

"We always want what we don't have, huh?" Chase tried a smile, but it appeared forced.

"Man, I'm sorry. I didn't mean it like that."

"You're lucky. You have two great parents. Maybe your dad just made a mistake."

"Look Chase, I'm sorry about earlier. I didn't mean it. I'm glad you're here. You're my best friend, and I should start treating you like one."

Chase got to his feet and went to the window, looking out. "Thanks. I'm going to go out for a bit. I'm sure you could use some time alone."

CHASE CROSSED the yard quickly. He did not want to be caught in Stacey's crosshairs. Even if she didn't know it was him, she was the last person he wanted to see right now. He rapidly crept around the side of the house and into the garage.

The small glass windows in the garage door let slivers of sunlight slip into the room, but it remained shadowy and dark. Chase made out a figure sitting motionless in the Porsche. "Nathan?"

Without a word, the figure opened the car door and emerged, a wilted shadow of his usually impressive six-four frame. "Hey, Chase."

"You okay?" Chase asked and barely registered a nod of the man's head. "I've been thinking—"

"Chase, Stacey knows," Nathan said and walked into a sliver of sunlight.

"Oh God," Chase gasped, wanting to run.

"She saw us this afternoon on the golf course," Nathan recounted calmly, as if mentioning a slight change in the weather.

"Oh my God," Chase repeated, shaking his head. "I'm so sorry."

Nathan put a hand on Chase's shoulder. "It's not your fault."

"But I never should have…. I don't know how I got so mixed up. All I wanted to do was help you."

"You did help," Nathan assured him.

"I ruined everything! I never should have come here this summer. I never should have come out. I'm so sorry." Chase brought his hands to his face, but not in time to keep the tears pressed inside.

Nathan pulled him into a hug. "Chase, this isn't your fault. If I would've had the courage to come out twenty years ago, none of this would be happening."

"But you also wouldn't have your family. They're worth so much more than this." Chase resisted the solace that Nathan's shoulder was providing for him and pushed away. "I'm leaving. If Tyler found out…."

Nathan grabbed on to his shoulders. "He won't. I'll fix this."

"I love him so much. I don't even know what I was thinking. I'm so sorry."

"It's okay, Chase. It's going to be okay."

Chase looked up at him and wanted to believe, wished he could believe what Nathan was saying was true. "What about you? Are you going to be okay?"

The man just smiled softly, and his eyes smiled with him, if a little sadly. "As good as I ever was. Maybe even a little better. Thank you."

"For what?"

"For the moment. It was beautiful," Nathan said and leaned in to kiss Chase good-bye.

And it was—beautiful. Chase knew that this was it, all it ever could be or was meant to be: one last kiss of comfort, courage, and parting.

The door flew open and light spilled into the garage. Nathan and Chase pulled apart and turned to see Tyler looking confoundedly from one to the other. "Dad?"

Chase took another step away from Nathan. "Tyler, this isn't what it looks like."

"Then what is it?" Tyler yelled and turned abruptly out of the garage.

Chase ran after him and onto the driveway, grabbing his shoulder. "Tyler, I can explain!"

"Don't touch me!" Tyler roared, shaking the hand from his shoulder.

"I'm so sorry. I didn't mean for this to…," Chase pleaded as Nathan arrived behind him.

"It's not Chase's fault, Tyler."

Tyler turned with rage on his father. "*You* stay out of this! I don't even know who you are!"

Chase tried to grab Tyler's shoulder again, determined to have his friend hear him out. "Tyler, please…."

"I said don't you fucking touch me!" Tyler turned and punched Chase, giving him a bloody nose. Chase recoiled momentarily and then tackled Tyler, pinning him to the ground.

Nathan jumped in and tried to pull them off each other. "Stop it!"

Stacey came running out of the house. "What's happening?"

Tyler pushed his father away from him and struggled to get back to his feet. "Get away from me!"

"Tyler, I didn't mean for—" Chase begged again.

"Shut up!" he spat. "You can leave, right now."

Chase was too ashamed to look at any of the Davidson family, and so he walked away, empty-handed and without a plan. He could still hear them behind him, though.

"Tyler…," Nathan tried his son one more time, but Tyler didn't respond.

Then, out of the corner of his eye, Chase saw Birdy run up the driveway from the neighbor's. "Why is everyone yelling?"

Without a word of explanation, Stacey took Birdy by the hand and quickly led her into the house.

THE LIGHTS in the Davidson family lake house stayed on late into the night while Nathan, Stacey, and Tyler stood in the living room circling around arguments, excuses, and resentful words in a symphony complete with crescendos, staccato accusations, and brief but welcome interludes of silence. Finally, it was Tyler, standing with his arms folded firmly across his chest, who broke the latest stillness that had descended. "But why did you stay, Dad?"

His father looked up at Tyler from where he had resigned himself to sitting in an easy chair, an easy and fixed target for their relentless questions and arraignment. "Because your mother was pregnant... with you."

"So, it's my fault?" Tyler asked, bewildered.

His mother lifted her head from where it rested on her fist and assured him, "Tyler, nothing is your fault. We stayed together because we thought it was best for both of us, and you."

"So, this... all of this... my parents, the family... it's all a lie?" Tyler asked, wiping away the tears forming at the edges of his eyes, too proud to let his parents see him cry.

"It's not a lie, Tyler. I love you, I love your mother," his dad reassured him. "I just had other feelings I'd never explored."

Tyler shot him a look laced with daggers. "So, my best friend is a fag and now my dad is a fag too."

His mother interrupted. "I know this is difficult, Tyler, but imagine what life would have been like without both of us...."

"Are you sticking up for him? Mom, you need to kick him out!"

She turned abruptly. Birdy was standing shyly against the doorframe. "Birdy! How long have you been standing there?"

"I'm hungry..." was all she responded, looking around at her family.

"All right, sweetheart. How about some pie? We should all have a piece of pie," his mom suggested and ducked into the kitchen.

Tyler watched in disbelief as his mother poured tea and dished out four slices of apple pie. The elephant seemed to be sucking all the oxygen from the room as she politely handed out the china cups and plates. Birdy cuddled up on their father's lap and stabbed a cinnamon-sprinkled apple slice with her fork contentedly. Tyler shook his head and unsuccessfully tried to hide his scorn from his younger sister. "Dad... this is bullshit." He pushed his plate away.

Birdy glanced at her father and then at Tyler's abandoned pie. "I like it. I'll have Tyler's piece."

Tyler stormed out before his tears could betray him again. If his sister's innocence could be protected, even for only a little while longer, he couldn't bear the thought of crushing it.

CHASE HUDDLED on a bus stop bench, shivering despite the summer night. He'd left the Davidsons' with only the clothes on his back and his pockets empty. His first choice would have been to grab the first bus out of town, but without his wallet he was stuck, directionless and full of regret. He tried to squeeze his eyes shut and block out the world, but it was really the storm on the inside that he sought shelter from.

Beams of light bled through his eyelids, and he brought his arm up to shield his face as he heard a truck rumble past. The engine slowed and he heard the friction of rubber on the pavement as the truck did a U-turn and bore back toward the bench. Lifting his arm, he squinted as the figure hopped out. "Chase? I thought that was you. Come on, let me give you a lift."

Without a plan of escape or a desire to spend the night on the uncomfortable bench, Chase stood with a modest smile of gratitude and walked toward the truck.

STACEY CLIMBED into Birdy's loft and knelt quietly beside her bed, watching her sleep. She gently stroked her daughter's hair and kissed her on the cheek. "You can sleep with me, Mommy," Birdy said groggily and lifted the covers for her mother. Stacey smiled thankfully and crawled in, holding the one part of her world that didn't seem to be ebbing away from her.

NATHAN LAY on the couch in the living room with a spare pillow and blanket snuck from the linen closet. There was no use in attempting to sleep, but he would at least adopt the position and hope by some miracle his mind would eventually shut off and allow some rest. Seeing the wooden box of family photos on the living room table, he reached for it and began flipping through the images. Unfortunately, they did little to give him comfort.

TUESDAY

WEDNESDAY

THURSDAY

FRIDAY

SATURDAY

SUNDAY

ON THE seventh night, Nathan was still sleepless on the couch. He stared at the ceiling and wondered what, if anything, he could do to reverse the pain he had caused. He knew he had no case to make; no testimony would warrant or validate his actions. He was fortunate that Stacey had moved forward, allowing him to coexist but with neither approval nor admonition, which was perhaps even worse. She had become distant, silent, and apathetic, seemingly drifting in her own thoughts, as if this physical reality were no more than a dream.

When Stacey appeared standing over him, he wasn't sure whether it was really her or his imagination. She gave him a solemn nod and then beckoned him to follow her into their bedroom.

Stacey was sitting on the end of their bed in an almost catatonic state, staring at her slippers, when Nathan slipped into the room. He stood waiting, holding his breath, unsure if he should be arming himself for a fight. Still staring at the floor, she patted the quilt with her hand, and so Nathan joined her on the end of the bed.

"I've rehearsed this so many times in my head. Before, I mean," she clarified. "And every time I was patient and understanding and calm. I'd tell you everything was okay, that it didn't change anything; that it didn't change us. And in time we'd grow closer because of it, because there was no more pretending, only truth. But last week changed things, obviously. And now that I'm sitting here, I don't know what to do."

"I never wanted you to get hurt," Nathan said.

"Nathan, I don't care that you're gay." Stacey finally found the courage to look up at him. "I care that you cheated on me and lied about it."

"I don't want you to leave, Stacey. I need you." Nathan sighed heavily. "I don't want to lose this."

"But what does that look like, Nathan? What will our life be?" Stacey asked. "Will you have boyfriends? Am I supposed to find a boyfriend?"

"I don't know that's what's right."

"But you want to be with a man."

"You're my best friend, Stacey, but there's always been something...."

Stacey stood and began pacing the room. "I know lots of married couples that *never* have sex. I don't think we've done so bad."

"We haven't, but there could be so much more for both of us."

Stacey turned on her heel and glared at him. "I don't need anything more. We made a commitment. I know you've made sacrifices, and so have I, but Birdy is ten years old and she needs both of us. She will have two parents. Nothing will jeopardize my family. Not me, not you, and certainly not him." She pointed accusingly out into the yard, as if Chase were lurking just outside their bedroom window. "It's up to you. I'm not leaving."

"What are you saying?"

"I'm saying it's your choice to stay or your choice to go," Stacey said, pulling her housecoat off its hook and wrapping it around herself.

Nathan hadn't expected this turn in the conversation. He hadn't expected that it would be his choice. He was guilty as charged, and he'd assumed she would just hand down a sentence. The weight of having a choice seemed almost too difficult to bear.

JAROD SAUNTERED shirtless out onto the second-story patio, his pajama bottoms hanging off his hips carelessly, though Chase barely noticed. Even as Jarod poured the morning coffee and his muscled chocolate torso paced in front of him, Chase all but ignored him. He rested his head on his interlaced hands on the tabletop, still regrettably silent.

"Hey, Chase, Jerry Springer called. He wants you on his show." Jarod tried a joke, but Chase wasn't ready to laugh over the incident.

"Honestly, I don't know how it got to that place. I just saw this man who so desperately was wanting to be himself...."

Jarod took the seat across from Chase and started fixing his coffee with cream and sugar. "I always wondered about Mr. Davidson."

"It's that look, right? I suspected something the minute I met him," Chase recalled, shaking his head.

Jarod grinned slyly and rested his hands behind his head. "I knew when you couldn't name even one player on the Steelers. That and the fact that your sneaker couldn't seem to keep itself away from mine."

"You were the one playing footsie with me!" Chase accused, and a smile crept across his face. He instantly sobered himself, feeling guilty for even momentarily coming out of his funk.

"I'm just sorry it took all that drama to get you over here for a few sleepovers."

Chase shot him a disparaging look.

"Okay, I know, I know. We've been over this and I'm sorry," Jarod said. "I was an ass, completely. I want to try again, on your terms. Out in the open."

Chase looked at him solemnly and shook his head. "You know I'm not ready for that. And neither are you."

"I'm not gonna say what you did was a smart move, but you're not the only one who made a mistake here, Chase. The blame doesn't completely land on your shoulders," Jarod said, standing and walking around the back of Chase's chair and massaging his neck. "Have you seen him yet?"

"Who?" Chase asked sarcastically.

"Tyler. It's been over a week. Don't you think you should talk to him?" Jarod asked, moving his hands down and kneading Chase's arms.

"I'm sure he doesn't want to see me."

"It's not going to get better all at once, but you have to start somewhere," Jarod advised. "You know you're welcome to stay with me here as long as you want. My parents went back to the city. It's our place now."

"Jarod, you don't have to do this...."

"I want to do this. Come on, as cute as you look wearing my clothes, it's time to get your stuff," Jarod said, pulling Chase out of his chair.

"I can't go there."

"We'll go together. I'm not gonna let anything happen to you." Jarod squeezed Chase's shoulder. "You can't hide from this forever."

JAROD MUST have seen the color drain from Chase's face as the truck pulled up beside the Davidsons' lake house. "You want me to go with you?"

Chase took a deep breath and shook his head. "I'll be okay, thanks."

"I'll be waiting right here," Jarod assured him with a smile.

Chase hopped out of the truck and crossed the yard to the guest cottage. He had no idea what he was going to say other than "I'm sorry." Those were the only words that continued to ring through his mind. He knew it was now or never. He knocked on the door and waited, fighting to keep his legs from turning around and walking him right back in the other direction.

No one answered.

Chase tried the doorknob. The door pushed open, and he peered inside. The guest cottage was empty. He quickly crossed to the open closet and saw that his clothes had been pulled from the hangers and shelves and stuffed haphazardly into his duffel bags. Thankful that this would save him time and a chance meeting with Tyler, which he really wasn't ready for, he slung the bags over his shoulder, grabbed his easel and canvases, and headed for the door.

Just as he was reaching for it, the doorknob turned, and the door swung open. Tyler breezed through but stopped in his tracks when he saw Chase. He gave him a once-over. His face turned to disgust as he saw the canvas pinched under Chase's arm, and he abruptly turned and left, slamming the door behind him. Chase glanced down and saw the painting of Nathan on the dock, banefully displayed in his hasty exit. He hurried out of the cottage and yelled after Tyler, but his breath was wasted. Tyler had apparently seen all he needed to see.

Chase trudged across the yard under the weight of his few belongings and down the driveway to Jarod's truck.

"Chase, wait."

He turned to see Nathan, oil rag in hand, exit the garage and take a few tentative steps toward him. But they had shared their good-bye already, and it had cost them dearly. There was nothing left to say, and any time spent in each other's company now could only further complicate matters and incriminate them. Chase paused, giving Nathan a grave smile, and nodded before turning and walking to Jarod's truck. He didn't know where his life was going to lead, but it wasn't supposed to be spent with Nathan.

KAYAKERS PADDLED across the lake in front of the pier as Stacey sat with her tea. The morning silence was only intermittently broken by the rhythmic slosh of the paddles slipping in and out of the water. Hearing the creak of the pier, she turned to see Tyler walking its length toward her. After reaching the bench where she sat surveying the lake, Tyler sat down beside her and laid his head on her shoulder.

"How'd you sleep?" she asked, resting a hand on his thigh.

"Not so good."

"It's going to be fine."

His gaze darted up to hers. "Fine?"

"You know what I mean. We've been through tough stuff before."

They sat in silence for a few moments, listening to the gentle waves lick against the lakeshore.

"So much for having the perfect family," Tyler remarked dryly.

Stacey smiled and patted his leg. "Perfect is overrated. Let's aim for functional, and we'll be one step closer to happy."

"I don't even know how I'm gonna look at Dad."

"He's having enough trouble looking at himself. He's still your dad; he's always been a good dad. This doesn't change that."

Tyler considered this for a few moments and then lifted his head from her shoulder. "Mom, did you know?"

Stacey looked at her son and smiled bravely. She didn't answer and she didn't need to. "I love your father, and we've had a good life together. You can't blame a person for who they are."

TYLER LAY in his bed and tossed a baseball up into the air, watching as it spun and fell back into his mitt. His eyes wandered over to the closet, where the empty wire hangers clinked together, dancing in the draft from the open window. There was a light knock on his door.

"It's open!"

His father slowly opened the door and nodded to him. Tyler looked away and went back to tossing the ball. "Tyler, can we talk?"

Tyler gloved the ball and sat up in his bed. "I'll go first. I hate what you did to Mom. I need you to know that."

"Tyler, I'm—"

"Let me finish. If you ever hurt her again, it'll be the last time you see any of us," he threatened.

"Okay."

Tyler sighed. Those words had been pent up inside him all week. Now that the anger had been channeled out of him, he looked at his father and searched for the empathy his mom had asked him to try to find. "I'm trying to understand it all, Dad."

"That's all I can hope for, thank you." He smiled and then his gaze drifted over to the other twin bed in the room. "Have you talked to Chase?"

"There's nothing to say," Tyler remarked coldly and went back to tossing the baseball up in the air.

"I know what I did was stupid," his dad admitted and grabbed the ball out of the air to get Tyler's full attention. "There's no excuse in the world that can change it, but I'm still your father. I'm the same guy I always was. I shouldn't have lied to your mother and I shouldn't have lied to you."

His father walked to the window and looked out. "When I met Chase, I realized what my life might have been like.... And it was exciting to think about. I wouldn't change the past. I'm not giving up on our family now, but it might look a little different. What happened with Chase wasn't his fault, and it doesn't change the fact that I love you very much, Tyler. Think about it, okay?" he asked as he tossed the ball back.

STACEY WATCHED as Birdy flipped through the colorful packages in the wood box and pulled out seeds for marigold and wisteria before handing them to her. They sat in the gazebo in the backyard, and Birdy had several pots of various sizes set out with her gardening gloves and trowel, ready to begin planting.

"Oooo... I like this one too," Birdy exclaimed, handing her a seed package for Stella de Oro daylily.

Stacey set her jaw firmly as she took the package. It was the same flower Chase had selected a week earlier, the one she had promised to plant as a perennial reminder. Well, everyone around here was going to learn to be a little flexible, including herself, she decided, and ripped the package open.

"Where did Chase go?" Birdy asked while slipping on her gloves.

"He's gone to stay somewhere else."

"Did he and Tyler break up?" she asked, as if this were the most probable scenario.

"Tyler and Chase were never dating."

"But they loved each other. I could tell." Birdy placed a seed on the end of her finger and pressed it into the soil.

"They loved each other like good friends. And right now, there are some issues they need to work out," Stacey explained, joining Birdy on the ground.

"Because Daddy kissed Chase?"

Stacey paused and looked at her little girl. She'd been working so hard at protecting her children, and here was evidence her efforts were in vain. Birdy stated it like a fact, with no judgment, just something that had happened.

"Yes, Birdy, because Daddy kissed Chase."

THE CAREFREE laughter of kids flying kites on the beach carried on the wind to where Tyler and Bre sat on a playground swing set. Neither made much use of the roped seats, just swaying gently and giving an occasional little push on the sand with a bare foot. The evening was wearing on, and the sky was beginning to lose the orange luster of sunset.

"Something on your mind?" Bre asked.

Tyler looked at her ruefully with a raised eyebrow. "You can tell?"

"Well, you haven't even tried to make out with me yet, and we've been here a solid ten minutes," Bre observed.

"I can't stop thinking about it. Why would Chase do that to me? What the hell was he thinking? What was my Dad thinking?"

"They obviously weren't thinking."

Tyler dug his foot into the sand to stop swaying and turned to Bre. "So what? Does that make it all right?"

"Tyler, this isn't about you. Try to imagine how hard it must have been for your dad. Maybe Chase was supposed to be here this summer."

"What the hell does that mean?"

"I'm just saying, if your dad is gay, he still deserves to be happy."

Tyler shook his head in disbelief. "How can my dad be gay?"

"Chase and your dad are still the same people."

"But why? Why would Chase do that to me?"

Bre sighed and looked pointedly at him. "I can't answer that for you, Tyler. Maybe you need to ask him."

They sat in silence for a while as the sky gathered more lavender into its lilac bouquet. Tyler couldn't imagine speaking to Chase, let alone forgiving him. It was hard enough pushing his mind to begin to accept his father. And here was Bre, who he had expected would be on his side, trying to suggest Chase was supposed to be here this summer. Here to what? Ruin his life, pull apart his family, and make his father gay? Yeah, that definitely seemed like something ripped from the pages of destiny. Tyler searched his heart for a shred of empathy but came up dry. There was no excuse for what they had done.

ACROSS THE lake, Stacey and Nathan were taking a walk, much as they had always done on summer evenings, although tonight felt acutely different to Stacey, as if each step were an accounting of summers past and only added more uncertainty to the future.

"Remember our first summer?" Nathan asked.

Stacey nodded. "We spoke of retiring out here one day. We were so excited."

"How's Birdy doing?"

Stacey sighed. "I think she knows. I don't think she understands it, but she doesn't have to, not yet. You haven't changed in her eyes."

"I love you, Stacey. You know that, right?"

Stacey walked along quietly for a moment. "I know. I just can't imagine what our life is going to look like. Will we still live together? If we did, will we get separate rooms? Maybe you should go home at the end of the summer and I can stay here...."

"I don't think we have the answers to those questions yet. We need to be there for Birdy. The rest—I think we take it a day at a time."

Stacey attempted a brave smile, but not having the answers scared her tremendously. If she didn't have the answers, how could she face their neighbors here or back in the city? There would be questions, without a doubt, and she'd prefer to be prepared for them. This was no longer a make-believe life, shrouded in politeness. This was the real thing, and she wasn't sure how to navigate its waters. The tears flooded her eyes without consent, and she fervently tried to wipe them away.

"Stacey, what is it?"

"I'm just... scared, Nathan. I'm thirty-six, with two kids and... well, what is my life supposed to be after this? I'll be alone, forever, really, because once Birdy leaves, then what will I have? It's not like I'm going to find someone else to be with now, at my age... and so I can just see my life stretching out in front of me—alone. It wasn't supposed to be this way." Stacey choked out the words, embarrassed at showing weakness. "I know we can't make any promises, not really, but if you could just make one... I'd just like to hope that you'll be my friend, no matter what happens."

Nathan took her hand in his, and they walked along the lake, knowing the journey ahead would not be an easy one, but whatever way the road wound, it would be easier to travel it together, at least as friends.

THE OIL paint was still glossy and wet in the morning sun as Chase wiped his hands on his T-shirt and slung it over his shoulder. He always found the morning light accentuated details he otherwise might have missed. There was no subject to study, however. He had been painting from memory, and the image there was as detailed as a photograph.

Jarod walked up behind him and said, "Looks great."

"It's getting there."

"No, it's there," Jarod said with a smile. "I'm feeling for some beach right now. What do you say?"

"Let's do it." Chase let his eyes wander over the portrait one last time. Unfortunately, his work didn't bring the satisfaction of accomplishment, but rather a twinge of bittersweet sadness.

WINDSURFERS SKIDDED across the whitecaps and a lone sailboat bobbed in the waves as Jarod's truck pulled up to the beach. Chase's face dropped as he hopped out and saw Tyler, Bre, and Christie huddled on beach blankets.

"You knew they'd be here?" he accused.

Jarod shrugged. "You can't avoid him forever."

Chase turned back to the truck. "I'm not going."

"I know it's scary, but you gotta try," Jarod said, grabbing his shoulders. "I'll be right here, but you gotta face this."

Chase paused a second, but he was out of fresh excuses. He nodded and his stomach turned to knots. He followed Jarod tentatively to the small cluster on the beach. Bre hopped up and reached out for hugs. "Hey, guys!"

Tyler glanced up and threatened, "This isn't a public party."

"Come on, let's just go," Chase implored Jarod, turning to leave.

"Ladies, I've got beer and snacks in the truck. Give me a hand?" Jarod asked, completely ignoring his request.

"Yeah, we'll help. Come on, Christie," Bre said, giving the other girl a significant look.

Chase took a step closer and sat in the sand. "Tyler, I'm sorry."

Tyler didn't look at him, keeping his eyes on the water. "Why'd you do it?"

"I was trying to help, and I messed up…."

"Trying to help?" Tyler glared at him incredulously.

"I don't have words that can fix this. I know you may not understand this, but what happened between me and your dad… it had nothing to do with you. I wasn't trying to break up your family. I thought that maybe I could help him be who he really is…." Chase stumbled over his words. He had so many thoughts, and it was hard to align them into any coherent sentences. "And then it went too far. I know that. I never meant for that to happen. And now I hate myself for it. If there was anything I could do to change it, I would."

Tyler didn't say a word. He stood up and walked away, leaving Chase alone on the beach. Chase had so much more to say, and yet he wondered if it would've been better if he hadn't spoken at all.

He had to leave. Whatever his dour purpose had been here, he'd screwed it up royally. There was no silver lining, no fast and easy lesson to be learned. He wondered at it, at the complex and yet plainly selfish nature of his actions. And as it was laid before him, he saw the gross and predictable psychology behind it all. This scared him the most because he'd always hoped he was something special, a one-of-a-kind rarity. But he wasn't. He was a self-indulgent human being willing to backstab his best friend to get what he wanted and then try to hide it. There was absolutely nothing special in that.

BIRDY RESTED the jack of hearts on the shoulders of the queen of diamonds and the two of spades. She pulled her hand away cautiously and then mime-clapped with excitement as the jack remained perched in his place in the house of cards. She sat cross-legged on the living room floor with Tyler and Bre, carefully crafting these unstable homes, doomed to crumble with the smallest tremor.

"What's going to happen, Tyler?" she asked.

"What do you mean?" Tyler looked at his sister while selecting another card from the deck.

"Will I ever see you again? After the summer?"

Tyler carefully set the nine of clubs in a teepee with the six of diamonds and winked at Bre conspiratorially. "Of course you will."

"But I never see Chase anymore. Since you guys broke up as friends, I never see him. If Mom and Dad break up, I'm scared I'll never see them again either."

Tyler rested a hand on Birdy's knee. "Mom and Dad might not split up. They might stay together. They don't know yet. They're talking it through."

Birdy drew another card from the deck and spun it thoughtfully between her fingers. "I think that's what you should do with Chase."

Bre looked from Birdy to Tyler and raised her eyebrows. She didn't have to say anything; the message was coming through loud and clear.

STACEY AND Nathan sat side by side on the wooden bench on the dock. Stacey turned and saw that her husband was silently crying. "You need to go, don't you?"

He looked at her and nodded, unable to bring himself to say it.

"I know...."

Nathan gritted his teeth and looked up at the sky as if another answer might be waiting there. "But Birdy...."

"She'll see you. We all will," Stacey assured him, placing a hand on his shoulder.

"I just need to find this piece of me...."

"And you need space to do it, I know." Stacey took a deep breath. "I guess we have to tell the kids."

They looked at each other, knowing it was the right answer, but knowing didn't make it any easier. Their gaze drifted to the lake house, taking in what was.

THE BLUE truck rumbled to a stop as it pulled up in front of the Davidsons'. They looked at each other for a second, and then Jarod gave Chase an encouraging smile. There wasn't going to be any immediate romance between them. Chase knew that. He had to get to a comfortable place with himself before even considering bringing someone into his mess. But when he was ready, he sure hoped he would find someone as supportive as Jarod. They'd both grown over the summer; maybe one day there'd be an opportunity for them to grow together. Chase returned the smile and hopped out, grabbing the canvas from the back of the truck.

He crossed the backyard and quietly climbed the stairs to the patio, resting the painting on a side table against the house. He set a small flowerpot in front of the painting to brace it and retraced his steps down the stairs and across the yard.

"Chase, wait…."

He turned to see Tyler standing in front of the guest cottage with his arms crossed. "Tyler—I was just…" he started but realized there was no use explaining. He doubted anything he said would make a difference at this point.

Tyler interrupted him, his voice low and quiet. "My dad's leaving."

Chase's eyes filled with tears, and there was nothing to say. "I'm really sorry, man."

"Me too. But I know now it wasn't your fault."

"Thank you. Tyler, I know I don't deserve it, but I miss you. I hope there's a day we can be friends again."

Tyler didn't budge.

"Okay, well, I better get going," Chase said and turned to leave.

"Take care of yourself, okay?" Tyler called after him. "Go Steelers, right?"

Chase turned and looked at his friend and knew he was getting the biggest gift he would ever receive. It was unwarranted, undeserved, and it broke his heart. He nodded and for the first time really understood what love was. "Go Steelers."

"Hey, everyone! Come look what I found!" Birdy yelled from the patio, and Tyler turned to go with a little wave.

Chase walked down the Davidsons' driveway and could hear them gathering on the patio. He hopped back in the truck and turned to Jarod. "I'm ready."

They drove in silence to the bus depot. Soon autumn would paint the passing trees with its red, orange, and yellow brushes, and all of this would fade like a dream as university classes began once again. The truck slowed to a stop, and Chase paused with his hand on the door latch. "Thank you, for everything."

"Not that we can go back and change things… but I wish I could," Jarod said, his hands firmly on the steering wheel.

"Yeah, me too," Chase said and hopped out of the truck, grabbing his duffel bags and easel from the back. He leaned back in the window before heading inside. "You know, we have a pretty good football team at school.… You should think about it. It's only a four-hour drive."

"You think they're looking for a gay running back?"

"I hope so." Chase turned and waved, and a seed of hope began to grow inside him that maybe, just maybe, they'd get a second chance at their first time.

THE DAVIDSON family gathered on the patio. No one said a word; they simply looked at the painting and the image reflected back at them. Chase had painted them how he'd seen them and how he'd hoped they'd remain: a vibrant, happy family.

"I don't want you to go, Daddy," Birdy said, reaching for her father's hand.

"I know. We'll see each other all the time, I promise," he said, pointing to the painting. "That's still us. It just might look a little different from time to time."

THAT NIGHT Nathan packed his car and drove back to the city. The road stretched out in front of him with infinite possibilities, but he was certain of one thing. He had to have his family in his life. Whatever came along on this journey of self-discovery would have to have room for them. They were everything to him and had given him the gift of a second chance. He vowed he wouldn't mess it up.

You've read the novel, now watch the film!

Receive a 50% discount on the rental or purchase of the film by entering promocode CharlieDavid at https://vimeo.com/ondemand/mulligansmovie

Q&A with Chip Hale—Director

How was directing your first feature different from other projects you've worked on?

Normally on independent films the director is usually the producer, writer, as well as craft service and a number of other positions. Which is something that I grew accustomed to, having worked on so many independent projects. However, for *Mulligans* I was just the director. I got to tell you it was nice to just do one job. I think it's something I can definitely get used to.

How did you personally relate to the screenplay?

The family really grabbed me when I first read *Mulligans*. The story has so many layers, but at each layer, the core is the family. Forgiveness isn't easy and each family member forgave Nathan for his choice in their own unique way.

What homage did you make to other films and filmmakers and incorporate into Mulligans?

Wow. That's a tough question. I feel like I'm the illegitimate "film-nerd" child of so many different filmmakers. I love how Soderberg and Paul Thomas Anderson use one shots often in their films. The confidence they have in the actors to just put the camera in place and let the actors act is something that influenced me during *Mulligans*. I did pay homage to Bull Durham in hopes to make the audience somewhat okay with Nathan and Chase's relationship. I'll keep my fingers crossed on that one.

Is there an overall message the film conveys in your opinion?

In my opinion the overall message is that most families are dysfunctional. To me dysfunctional is the norm, especially in today's society. I feel *Mulligans* reminds people that no matter how dysfunctional their family may be, there are other families that are similar if not almost identical.

Do you make an appearance, or a Hitchcock cameo in Mulligans?

I do make a Hitchcock-type cameo, but I'm not going to tell you where. You have to find it.

Do you have a favorite sequence or scene?

There are so many, and my favorite changes every time I watch the film. Right now my two favorite scenes are when Chase comes out to Tyler at the golf course. Derek and Charlie are great in this scene; both of their performances are so real. The other is when Nathan and Chase finally get together. It's such an uncomfortable moment, but Alice (the cinematographer) and I shot it to look pretty to get that juxtaposition. I'll keep my fingers crossed on that one as well.

Q&A with Actor Dan Payne—Nathan Davidson

What drew you to the role of Nathan?

It isn't very often you get the chance to play a character with so much depth and conflict—what an amazing opportunity for exploration and insight. I wanted to challenge myself to tell this great story through this character and deal with the internal and external roller coaster of obstacles his journey presents.

How did you approach the infatuation that grows with the character of Chase?

I approached it like every infatuation I've ever felt! You have an attraction/connection with someone, you let the seed get planted in your mind, then you rationalize it to death and tell yourself no one will get hurt; you begin to see more and more great qualities and freedom in indulging in that emotion and feeling—and in that person. Then you jump!

You were involved in an earlier live reading of the script through the Cold Reading Series—what parts of Nathan do you relate to?

I related to the feeling of getting older! I could also remember times in my life that I was living it for others and thinking it was the "right thing to do" to keep people happy. Unaware that it was a false sense of happiness that resided on thin ice. It reminded me that being true to myself and honest with the people I care about will always be the "right thing to do." That path gives love foundation.

Why do you feel it's important to tell this story?

Love is universal. And there is a universal struggle to find love and acceptance that starts with being honest with yourself. You have to find that in order to find peace and happiness for you and those around you!

Q & A with actress Thea Gill—Stacey Davidson

There are many elements in the role of Stacey that are very different from Thea Gill. How do you approach a role in order to bridge the gap between who you are and who the character is?

I try to approach acting as a way to know myself better. I'm discovering that the whole process IS like a bridge actually—a passageway to unknown places within. I work very hard to remain professional on set so the character I'm finding has some sort of safety net, and it also makes the masochistic nature of the search bearable… because Crafty always made me special treats!

There are some extremely powerful turns of events in the world of Stacey. What message do you hope audiences will walk away with?

I suppose there's a desire in me to see *Mulligans* be a comfort to those who most who need it, to be cathartic, to be a feel-good film, and to take the guilt of making mistakes away….

You have an illustrious history working within LGBT film and television. As a straight woman do you feel a connection to help with visibility of this community?

I was surrounded by girls at CHS, the private girls' school I attended in Vancouver, BC, since I was six years old and recently celebrated my thirty-eighth birthday with girls from all over the world at Dinah Shore in Palm Springs, CA! I genuinely feel I have been called upon to focus a great deal of my life to the study and activism of lesbian and gay rights. I always will.

Q & A with Actor Derek James—Tyler Davidson

The role of Tyler was written specifically for you…. How did you approach the role?

Well it didn't take too much. Luckily having been friends with Charlie for the last eight years I figured if he wrote Tyler for me to play, he was basically writing my personality in a different situation. So I just had fun with it.

Mulligans *was shot entirely in your hometown of Victoria, British Columbia. Was it exciting to return to shoot a film?*

It was very cool. It felt so comfortable to be there—it helped my performance. Plus I knew I would ALWAYS someday get to go back to shoot something, so it was awesome it was my buddy's film. That HE wrote! Crazy.

You have one of the most quotable lines in the film—"Go Steelers." Do you feel that guys generally have a difficult time showing their love for each other?

I think EVERYBODY has a hard time showing their love for one another. Really, the words don't matter, right? It's the intent behind them. Funny thing about the "Go Steelers" line is that neither Charlie nor I like the Steelers or know anything about the Steelers. Or football for that matter!

What do you think the overall message of the film is?

People are who they are. And it takes more effort to hate people than it does to love them. Plus I don't know too many people that say "Oh man. I wish I hadn't have wasted all that time loving that person."

Q&A with Charlie David—Writer, Producer, Chase

What inspired the story of Mulligans?

My producing partner, Linda Carter. Linda is also my manager, and when I was making the decision to come out as an actor she gave me some sage advice. She said, "You will lose some roles by coming out and you'll get some roles for coming out. What we can do is create your own work—so start writing."

That was basically it. Then I began to write concepts that involved my best friend Derek James and myself. *Mulligans* originally started as kind of a frat humor comedy. Then obviously as I explored the relationship and the family, which is completely invented, I discovered a much richer, interesting story.

How did you juggle the roles of screenwriter, actor, and producer?

It definitely wasn't easy! One of my heroes is Warren Beatty, and he has a career I aspire to in terms of being involved in the creative and business sides of his projects. I found that the aspects of bringing together a creative team, financing the production, and planning a rollout for distribution were all very exciting for me. As exciting as getting in front of the camera and acting.

There were definitely some days, especially in the last two weeks of preproduction that I thought I was going to implode. Fortunately we assembled a fantastic and supportive team of problem solvers which allowed me to prioritize where my attention was most needed at any given time.

What were the challenges of bringing together your first film?

There were many! Taking on a large-scale project for the first time has many challenges. There is the educational arc of learning the different aspects of production; there is the catch-22 aspect of securing talent and crew in order to secure financing but needing financing in order to secure talent! Being a producer I've found is all about relationships, and trust me, a lot of people came to the table to assist with this project. We were extremely fortunate in so many areas from our cast working for much less than their quotes, donated locations, wardrobe sponsorships, deals cut on almost everything you'll see in the film.

There's most likely an interesting story about generosity in almost every actor, crew member, prop, location, and shot.

Why was it important for you to tell this story?

It's hard to say whether I was directly influenced by the story I'm telling or whether by telling the story I am a more open conduit to related topics. In either case I have heard so many stories from people in similar situations where a member of the family comes out and how the family unit is affected. In this case with the story really focusing on the parents, I thought it was interesting to watch someone who's already created a life for themselves in terms of profession, family, and children have second thoughts about who they were and why they'd come to the reality they created for themselves.

Beyond this I feel there is a great need for representing different aspects of the LGBT community. There is a flood of entertainment that reflects a small section of the gay experience, and I wanted to explore some new terrain. *Mulligans* is about a family and the very human needs of loving each other, but also loving ourselves enough to want to live our authentic selves.

Which role was easiest to write? The hardest?

As a writer there are always triggers inside the people I create that remind me of someone in my real life. The role of Tyler came extremely quickly because I based a lot of it on my relationship with Derek James, my best friend. His rhythm of speech and comic sensibility was just there—innate.

The role of Stacey was extremely fun and pulls from several different women I respect in my life. The role of mother is fascinating to me in its complete and general loss of the sense of self that occurs with raising children. Stacey has a very precise and methodical way of speaking; she lives in her head and believes her efforts to create a perfect exterior and perfect Martha Stewart-like home will transform the loneliness she feels.

She's also an interesting dichotomy of, at a fundamental level, knowing the truth about her husband but living in such extreme denial.

The role of Birdy was a complete fabrication, and so in many ways was maybe one of the most entertaining to explore. I created her as a sort of sage beyond her years—she speaks on a very adult level much of the time but doesn't necessarily realize how on the money she is with her remarks.

The role of Nathan was perhaps the most difficult for me to create. In some ways this may have been because he is the man that I could have been; the man that represents for me the path not taken in my own life. I was definitely pulled to write his experiences but strangely maybe had the narrowest grasp of what it really means to be this person.

Okay, I lied! Maybe the most difficult role to write was that of my own—the role of Chase. There is a temptation to create the hero out of your own role. This was a strong pull but one that proved to be the incorrect motivation for the story. *Mulligans* is about the family and the parents specifically. The role of Chase is really the catalyst—he is the inciting incident that propels everyone into a journey of self-discovery, but it is not the story of Chase. So in essence trying to create the secondary antihero in the role of Chase—giving him enough redeemable qualities so as not to be contemptible in the eyes of the audience but not without his degree of fault in the whole matter.

Q & A with Linda Carter—Producer

Why was it important for you to make this film?

Well, it was my first film.... I'd been talking about making a film for a long time, and taking that first giant leap was a challenge. It's easier to talk about it, than actually do it—but not near as much fun. When I read the script I really felt it was an interesting story, and one that I had not seen before. I also felt it had good roles for some of the folks I represent, and so I was motivated and excited!

What were the challenges of shooting on location?

Being that we were a low-budget film presented many challenges. When it came to locations, there was some renegade shooting involved... run in, get the footage, get out... don't tell anyone! A lot of our days were spent at the cottage that belonged to a friend of a friend. With a bigger budget we would have been able to put them up in a hotel and take over the property till we were done, but alas, we had to put the house back every night so they could live in their house, and return each day and take it apart again. Time-consuming, more room for breakage, continuity errors, etc. And of course, the location we chose, as beautiful as it was, happened to be on a flight path and very near a dog kennel... so there was a lot of... "Can you go to that house across the lake and see if they would take their dog inside?"

How long has the process been from first draft of script to final product?

Gee, I think I'm too old to remember. I know we spoke about the story way, way back in 2001 when I first mentioned wanting to shoot a film... and the first draft didn't get to me for a couple of years... then we had it presented at the Cold Reading Series in Vancouver and that solidified for me it was the right film to make, but it needed rewrites... so the next two years were a succession of changes and evolution and now we have a finished product!

What excites you about the filmmaking process as a producer?

Almost everything! I love it. Using both sides of my brain is great. It is a real gift being able to be a part of the creative side, and I also love the business side—so for me it really is a good fit. I also found it fascinating how the product itself evolved as each creative entity joined in and brought their thoughts and genius to the project. It is such a wonderful collaborative venture.

What moment stands out for you as magic?

There is more than one, but I remember very vividly, it was day one or two, and most of the cast and crew were standing in the driveway of the cottage. Because this was such a low-budget film, many of those gathered were friends and family, which only made it more special. The crew were putting the car mount on the car, under the watchful brilliant eye of Alice, our cinematographer, and Chip, the director, was in his zone—everyone was laughing and having fun. I forced myself to stop for a few minutes and just take it all in. It was very emotional for me; I choked back tears—and then carried on, but I loved the feeling… can't wait to do it again!

CHARLIE DAVID has hundreds of hours of film and television to his credit predominantly exploring the LGBTQI2S experience. He has been selected as the Canadian Filmmaker in Focus by the Kashish Film Festival in Mumbai, India, an invited guest of the Canadian embassy in South Africa to share his documentary on HIV+ youth, executive produced Beyond Gay: The Politics of Pride, a global look at pride celebrations and winner of multiple awards including the HBO Best Doc award at the Miami International LGBT Film Festival. Charlie was nominated for a Golden Sheaf Award for Drama for Pygmalion Revisited, one of the episodes of his scripted TV miniseries Shadowlands based on the his book of short stories.

For more information and to connect, please visit border2border.ca

Books by Charlie David

Mulligans

Boy Midflight

Shadowlands

Published by
BORDER2BORDER ENTERTAINMENT
www.border2border.ca

This is a work of fiction. Names, characters, places, and incidents either are the product of author imagination or are used fictitiously, and any resemblance to actual persons, living or dead, business establishments, events, or locales is entirely coincidental.

Mulligans © 2008 Charlie David.

All rights reserved. This book is licensed to the original purchaser only. Duplication or distribution via any means is illegal and a violation of international copyright law, subject to criminal prosecution and upon conviction, fines, and/or imprisonment. Any eBook format cannot be legally loaned or given to others. No part of this book may be reproduced or transmitted in any form or by any means, electronic or mechanical, including photocopying, recording, or by any information storage and retrieval system, without the written permission of the Publisher, except where permitted by law. To request permission and all other inquiries, contact Border2Border Entertainment www.border2border.ca

Mulligans
© 2020 Charlie David.

Library of Congress Control Number: 2015920902
Published June 2020
v. 3.0

First Edition published by Palari Publishing LLP, 2010.
Second Edition published by Dreamspinner Press LLP, 2016.

Printed in Great Britain
by Amazon